Cover Copy

Traveling through time…for a Highlander.

It's been four long years since Arianna MacLeod Cunningham's ancestor opened a portal in the past to free lost souls and inadvertently pulled Arianna through from the future into her time. Arianna desperately wants to save her ill father and return to him, and when she travels to the Highland Games being held so near her childhood home, that desire is one she can no longer deny.

Highland warrior James MacDonald is at the Games representing his clan. He hopes to topple the reigning champion, although the last thing he expects is to fall under Arianna's spell. She's the girl he cared for when she first fell through time, and now four years later, the woman he can't allow to walk away.

When Arianna seeks to send a message to her father, James comes to her aid, only now destiny is about to pull them both apart. Can James find a way to save the woman he loves...even through the separation of time?

Books by Joanne Wadsworth

The Matheson Brothers Series
Highlander's Desire, Book One
Highlander's Passion, Book Two
Highlander's Seduction, Book Three
Highlander's Kiss, Book Four
Highlander's Heart, Book Five
Highlander's Sword, Book Six
Highlander's Bride, Book Seven
Highlander's Caress, Book Eight
Highlander's Touch, Book Nine
Highlander's Shifter, Book Ten
Highlander's Claim, Book Eleven
Highlander's Courage, Book Twelve
Highlander's Mermaid, Book Thirteen

Highlander Heat Series
Highlander's Castle, Book One
Highlander's Magic, Book Two
Highlander's Charm, Book Three
Highlander's Guardian, Book Four
Highlander's Faerie, Book Five
Highlander's Champion, Book Six
Highlander's Captive (Short Story)

Billionaire Bodyguards Series
Billionaire Bodyguard Attraction, Book One
Billionaire Bodyguard Boss, Book Two
Billionaire Bodyguard Fling, Book Three

Books by Joanne Wadsworth

Regency Brides Series
The Duke's Bride, Book One
The Earl's Bride, Book Two
The Wartime Bride, Book Three
The Earl's Secret Bride, Book Four
The Prince's Bride, Book Five
Her Pirate Prince, Book Six

Princesses of Myth Series
Protector, Book One
Warrior, Book Two
Hunter (Short Story - Included in Warrior, Book Two)
Enchanter, Book Three
Healer, Book Four
Chaser, Book Five

Highlander's Champion

Highlander Heat, Book Six

JOANNE WADSWORTH

Highlander's Champion
ISBN-13: 978-1-99-003427-5
Copyright © 2015, Joanne Wadsworth
Cover Art by Joanne Wadsworth
First electronic publication: February 2015

Joanne Wadsworth
http://www.joannewadsworth.com

AUTHOR'S NOTE:
This book is a work of fiction. The names, characters, places, and incidents are products of the writer's imagination or have been used fictitiously and are not to be construed as real. Any resemblance to persons, living or dead, actual events, locale or organizations is entirely coincidental. The author does not have any control over and does not assume any responsibility for third-party websites or their content.

Published in the United States of America

First digital publication: February 2015
First print publication: February 2015

Dedication

For my precious family.

Acknowledgements

I have an incredibly supportive family who allow me so much time to write. Huge thanks go to my hubby, Jason, and kiddies, Marisa, Caleb, Cruise and Rocco. Hugs.

For my readers, I can't thank you enough for joining me, and taking this journey to where imagination and magic soar.

Samuel Cunningham

The battlefield on the Isle of Lewis, Scotland, 1569.

As the cold of night fully descended, Samuel Cunningham stood amongst the MacLeod of Dunvegan's warriors within the forest bordering a field swirling with tendrils of fog. Their enemy awaited them on the other side, a good hundred MacKenzie warriors in battle attire, their torches lit and staked into the ground.

Tormod, the Chief of MacLeod, stormed back and forth before his captains, fury riding him hard. "'Tis time to take the castle of Stornoway back. This is our kin's MacLeod land and no invaders will steal it. Samuel, you're to lead our right wing, John, the left, and the remainder of us will hold the center. We hit them hard, advancing as one once the hour of truce has passed." He halted and eyed Anna MacLeod, their healer and the mother of Samuel's betrothed, Zenia. "Anna, you're to return to camp with one of my guardsmen. I willnae have you caught up in the middle of this battle."

"You need every warrior at your side, Chief. I can make my own way back," she pleaded.

"Nay, Anna. I gave Zenia my word no harm would come to

you. Your daughter needs—"

A thundering roar reverberated as the MacKenzies plowed across the battlefield, breaking the truce well before its time.

"All to arms." Tormod shoved his sword high in the air and bellowed, "We fight, for justice and freedom. Let us take these blackguards down."

Samuel raced through the underbrush along the line of MacLeod warriors to the right, hauled his claymore from his scabbard across his back and released a bloodcurdling battle cry. He and the right wing rushed forward and into the fray of fierce MacKenzies.

He swung and fought, sweat pouring from his body just as his clansmen did the same. In the dark, the sound of men grunting and fighting echoed all around. They had to win this war. They fought not only for their MacLeod kin here on Lewis, but also to keep their enemy from bringing their war to Dunvegan's shores. He'd never allow any harm to come to the woman he loved, the woman he intended to wed the moment he returned to her.

He slashed toward the center, inching closer toward Tormod.

"Be prepared to die." A warrior came at him and Samuel blocked the MacKenzie's swift blow. Their claymores clashed dead center, steel ringing loud against steel. Another MacKenzie swung and struck Samuel's ribs. Pain ricocheted through him and he staggered back from the brutal blow. Two against one. Damn bloodthirsty MacKenzies. They fought dirty.

Breath ragged, he collapsed to his knees. Blood covered the padded armor of his steel-studded war coat, the blood of the warriors he'd slain now mingling with his own. He clutched his side and tried to stem the flow but his life-force poured through his fingers.

"Samuel!" A woman's cry rang out and Anna hurried from the darkened tree tine clutching her brown woolen kirtle's skirts.

"Nay, stay back, Anna," he rasped and spat out a mouthful of blood. The metallic taste coated his tongue and pervaded the air. She should've returned to camp.

"Where are you hurt?" She fell to her knees in front of him, her long red-gold locks, the same beautiful shade as Zenia's, bundled under a woolen cap.

"My side. There's naught you can do." He tried to heave to his feet but fell and slumped onto his back.

Anna shoved his war coat up and gasped. "You must live, Samuel. Zenia needs you." She glanced across the field littered with bodies and warring men, "Tormod. Hurry, come. I cannae heal this."

Tormod struck the MacKenzie he fought with one brutal blow of his blade then sprang over the fallen to Samuel's side. He dropped to one knee and grasped his forearm. "Hold fast, Samuel."

"I cannae leave Zenia." The chilly air invaded his limbs.

"I'll do what I can." Tormod raised his hands and called forth his great gifted skill. "With the power of my ancestral MacLeod fairy blood, I wish for a portal to open. Allow Samuel to seek the light and journey to where he shall find peace and aid. Send him swiftly on his way and return him again one day."

A fierce wind whipped around Samuel and a swirling vortex opened.

Anna scampered backward in the slick grass and knocked into a slain MacKenzie. The enemy's breath rattled in his chest, blood coating his face and obscuring his eyes as he lifted one fisted hand. A dagger gleamed in the moonlight then he plunged his weapon down and Anna screamed.

"Nay!" Samuel heaved up but fell away into the churning dark abyss. It took him, heart, body, and soul.

Arianna's Arrival

Seventeen years later, approaching the bridge over the Cairn Water, near Glencairn Castle, Scotland, 1586.

Death pervaded this place where murder had struck. Zenia MacLeod crouched and pressed her palm against the gritty soil lining the old carriage route bordered with lime trees. The earth shook and the wind rustled the fallen autumn leaves into a swirling mass of reds and burnt oranges. 'Twas midday yet the skies overhead darkened as if night were about to fall.

Eyes closed, Zenia reached out with her healer's senses and searched. The souls that had recently passed in this place still lingered with nowhere to go and their desperate call for help ricocheted deep inside her. Some might brand her a witch, but her soul glowed with light, her gifted skill used only to help those who asked for her aid and these lost souls did.

Standing, she raised her hands and called forth her skill. "With the power of my ancestral MacLeod fairy blood, I wish for a portal to open. Free these displaced souls in need of aid and allow them to seek the light."

The wind whistled through and whipped her blue skirts about her legs. Stars shimmered all around and those lost souls in need streaked toward the light and through the portal.

To further aid them on their way, she made another wish. "May your journey take you to where your light shines brightest and you long to be. Find the peace you seek."

The portal's swirling vortex began to close then slowed as a blazing star streaked through. The star crashed into the bushes along the roadside as the portal shimmered shut. This had never happened before. She hurried to the scrub and knelt as the bright light dispersed. A lass of mayhap seven and ten, her long golden blond tresses crackling with energy lay sprawled within the springy leaves of brushwood. She remained motionless, not a breath escaping her, then she gasped, her chest suddenly rising and falling as she slumped to her side once more.

Zenia fluttered her hand close to the lass's mouth and her breath warmed her palm. The girl lived, although strange clothing clung to her body, the shiny white fabric holding strands of gold woven within. She plucked the shiny thread which stretched then rebounded back onto her. Unusual, although no matter where the lass had come from, she clearly needed her aid. Zenia set to work and examined her for injury. Her knees and elbows were covered in grit and her right leg and arm, bent at a terrible angle, would cause her great pain when she realigned her limbs. 'Twas just as well the girl remained unaware.

"I saw bright lights!" a warrior called as he rode across the bridge, his shoulder-length locks of auburn brushing the massive two-handed claymore holstered to his back. He pulled his horse to a halt and jumped down. "Is someone hurt?"

"This lass here is injured."

"Where did she come from? She seemed to appear from the lights."

"She did, and she came through a portal I open—" She shouldn't speak so freely. He wasn't one of her clansmen who'd seen her skill rise when she called it forth, except a sense of trust shimmered through her and it was strong.

"I hold only respect for the gifted." The warrior eyed her. "There's naught to fear from me. You said you opened a portal?"

She gave into her instinct, and said, "Aye, 'twas a portal she came through. I'm Zenia MacLeod." She stroked the lass's long blond locks back from her face as a surge of protectiveness rose. "She needs aid and I must do all I can to help her."

"Who is she?"

"I've no idea." She untangled the girl's hair from around a silver chain at her neck and lifted a charm free. Engraved upon the disk was an image of the unicorn, the same mythical creature that graced her own paternal Cunningham clan crest. She turned the charm over and smoothed her thumb over the words etched upon the back.

Arianna MacLeod Cunningham.
DOB: 1998.

"Her name is Arianna."

The warrior knelt next to her in his black leather trews and tan padded cotun and inspected the inscription. "It says her date of birth is the year nineteen ninety-eight. That cannae be right."

"Aye, 'tis of a time over four-hundred years from now."

"She isnae dressed like any lass I've seen." He frowned. "Although, I've heard tales of a skill like yours. It runs deep through your MacLeod line, no' that I've ever met one of your kin who has it."

"'Tis a rare ability and I only speak of it amongst my closest, or those I sense I can trust."

"What happened here to cause you to open a portal?"

"There were so many who'd recently passed and I heard their call for aid. When I opened the portal, they flew toward the light, although I've never had one of flesh and blood arrive. She's the first to ever travel to me." She grasped his hand. "Please, you cannae speak of this to another. No' all understand as you do."

"You have my word I'll keep your secret. I would never bring harm to one so gifted." He turned his gaze on the lass and gently cupped her cheek. "She's alive and now in need of aid. I'll gladly do all I can."

"Then she has come to the right place, where her soul desired and her light shines brightest. I thank you for your offer and will gladly accept your help." She covered his hand with hers and looking deep inside her mind, searched to ensure he was all he'd proclaimed to be. Aye, his strength was undeniable, and he held great honor. That knowledge satisfied her. "Your name, kind sir?"

"James MacDonald, from clan MacDonald on the Isle of Skye."

"You are a long way from home."

"Aye, I'm traveling to Edinburgh and sailed by way of the Firth of Clyde. My chief has sent me on his behalf to speak to the king." He swayed, planted both hands on the ground and squeezed his eyes shut. "I see something, a vision. Do you see it?"

A vision shimmered to life and she closed her eyes and embraced what was to come.

The girl before them raced out of a tall building, one not made of stone, but instead built of metal and glass. Arianna glanced back at the sign above the building. The wooden plaque proudly displayed the name *Isle of Skye Dance Studio*. Giggling, she twirled a pair of dainty white slippers in her hand as she stepped onto a thoroughfare of stony black. The path wasn't one that conveyed horse and cart but machines made of steel with wheels. One slammed into Arianna and she flew over the top and landed in a crumpled heap. As the machine screeched to a halt, the lass's form flickered and disappeared. Gone. And now she was here in the past.

Zenia opened her eyes as the warrior did the same. "My

apologies. Somehow I connected the three of us when I touched you and you saw her plight as I did."

"She most certainly comes from the future." He shook his head and blinked. "What I saw was far beyond this place. A large contraption on wheels hit her. Do you experience such visions often?"

"From time to time. She's clearly a lost soul, and her charm tells me she is of both clans, MacLeod and Cunningham, just as I am." She touched her chest. As blood of her blood, she would watch over the lass sent to her. "I'm the healer of clan Cunningham. I live in a cottage in these woods near the Earl of Glencairn's residence, and I need to remain with her. If you would, could you please follow the stream a furlong or two along the forest trail until you reach my cottage then bring me the basket of healing herbs and supplies sitting beside my front door?"

"Aye, I'll be as quick as I can." He bounded onto his black destrier and urged his mount between the trees either side of the thickly forested path.

Thanks heavens she would have this warrior's aid. She shoved her long red-gold locks over her shoulder and collected some sturdy sticks of just the right length. She tore a piece of cloth from the hem of her blue woolen kirtle and as carefully as she could, realigned Arianna's arm and leg. She bound the girl's limbs in place with the sticks and cloth, just as her mother, Anna, had taught her so many years ago.

The warrior returned and rode to her side, jumped down and looped his horse's reins over a low branch. "I have what you asked for." He set her basket on the ground and cupped the girl's cheek. "She's warm and still lives."

"Aye. She is strong even though injured." She cleaned the girl's scrapes and wounds, applied a salve to keep her clear from any infection then directed James to carry Arianna's limp body back to her home.

The child would heal and survive.

She'd make certain of it.

Clan Cunningham

Two months later, at Glencairn Castle, the residence of the seventh Earl of Glencairn.

Zenia folded her hands in her lap as she sat in the earl's solar.

"Why have you come to me, Zenia?" Cunningham eased back in his chair before the grandly carved desk the old earl had sat behind.

"When I came to you after my mother's death, you offered me sanctuary and ensured I had a home and for that I am most grateful."

"My clan needed a healer and you have served us well over the years. I had no doubt you would after coming to us from the Chief of MacLeod's home. Is this visit about the lass you healed who came through one of your portals?"

"William told you?"

"Aye. He mistook her at first for one of his own sisters, which I find hard to believe."

William, the earl's eldest son, was a strong warrior who excelled with the sword. He'd come across Arianna the week before in the woods as she'd taken a walk. Each day she'd gained more strength and when William had returned with Arianna to her cottage, the three of them had spoken of all that had happened. Zenia had naught to hide from her own clansmen, and she'd known then it would only be a matter of time before she spoke to the earl about Arianna.

"William did mistake her. She is almost identical to the twins, and so too is she ten and seven as your daughters are." Arianna deserved all she could possibly provide for her, which was why she was here. "The lass is kin to me, just as she is kin to you. Her name is Arianna MacLeod Cunningham."

"So William told me, and that she hails from the Cunninghams on the Isle of Skye, your place of birth." He rested his elbows on his desktop and tapped his fingertips together. "What is it about her that convinces both you and William she comes from the future?"

"You need only speak to her yourself to see the truth." She cleared her throat. "Excuse me. I didnae mean to be so forthright."

"'Tis fine." His steely-gray gaze narrowed. "William also tells me there's a MacDonald warrior on my land. The two of them fought."

"James MacDonald was passing through on his way to Edinburgh and witnessed Arianna's arrival. He aids me as he can but must soon continue on with his travels. His trip has been delayed by several weeks and his chief awaits his return on Skye after he visits with the king." She fidgeted with the pleats in her forest green skirts. The Cunninghams and the MacDonalds rarely got along. "James gave the lass his offer of protection, and she is such a delight."

"You've become attached to the child?"

"Aye. She also enjoys learning my craft and is a natural with the healing herbs. I'm here this day because I have a request."

"Then speak freely, Zenia." The morning sun broke through

the thick layer of cloud outside and filtered through the window. It played over the papers and the pile of seneschal's accounts set neatly to the side of the earl's desk.

"Arianna needs a home such as yours. I cannae provide for her all she will need."

"You wish for me to bring her into my household? My, my." He leaned back, his chair creaking as he did. "That is a bold request."

"She has incredible knowledge to offer. She also left behind a father she loved. She has no one and I brought her into this time and have been unable to return her. I've tried, so many times, but my ability to open a portal only rises for those souls who've already passed, or those who hover on the edge of death as she did. I fear she is here to stay."

"Even as bold as your request is, I am intrigued." He tapped the polished oak desktop. "I would need to meet her afore I could make a decision."

"Most certainly." Hope bloomed in her chest. "She awaits outside."

"Then by all means, bring her in."

She dashed to the thickly paneled door and opened it. Arianna stood in the darkened hallway in a simple gown of brown, one she'd embroidered for her along the ruffled neckline with gold thread to match her long golden locks.

"Is all well?" Her big blue eyes asked so much more.

"Come in, my dear. The earl will see you." She squeezed Arianna's hands then motioned her through.

Arianna entered and dipped her head at Cunningham. "It's lovely to meet you, my laird."

"Hell." He shoved to his feet and yanked on the front of his gray tailored jacket. "You are as I've been told. I can barely tell the difference between you and my daughters."

"The man at your door got quite the surprise when I arrived." Arianna shuffled from slippered foot to foot on the burgundy woolen mat before his desk.

"Take a seat and tell me all about this time in the future you're from. Your speech certainly isnae as thick as mine."

"I was born in the year nineteen ninety-eight and lived on the Isle of Skye with my father." She sat on one of the three navy and black striped padded chairs set in a half circle. "He fashions weapons of old and sells them all around the world, or will, in the future. His name is Samuel Cunningham. He's all I have."

Zenia had been quite shocked when Arianna had first spoken her father's name, although her surprise had quickly passed. Samuel was a common name, and so was Cunningham. The child's kin also came from Skye where names were more often than not handed down from generation to generation.

"There are a number of Cunninghams on Skye, all from my clan. Tell me about the future." Eagerly, he walked around his desk, moved his quill and ink bottle and perched on the front edge.

"In the future all children attend school from a very early age, both girls and boys alike. I just completed my final year of secondary school and recently enrolled at the University of West Scotland to further my studies."

"You're well educated?"

"Very well educated."

"What of your mother?"

"I never knew her, although I bear her name. She too was called Arianna and was a MacLeod. She died not long after I was born and Dad's been fighting an illness called cancer these past few months."

"Is this illness one he might perish from?"

"If he'd discovered his illness a little earlier, he could have easily caught it in time. His chances right now are half and half." Tears welled in her eyes and she blinked them away. "I've written him a letter, one I need you to hold onto and ensure he receives in the future. His address is on the outside and the date it must be delivered to him by. I've warned him about his cancer and told him as much as I could." She pulled a piece of parchment folded in three from her pocket and handed it to the earl. "Will you keep it safe for me and ensure he receives it?"

"Aye, I'll do all I can, but you're asking me to ensure he receives this in a time over four-hundred years from now." He took her letter and inspected the address on the outside. "He lives in Dunvegan Village?"

"A few miles north of it, yes. Our home is close to Dunvegan Castle, right along the cliffs."

"There is a large parcel of land there owned by the Cunninghams and several families in my clan call that stretch of Skye home."

"My father's ancestors live there now."

"Then you are indeed kin." He crossed to a tall chest with ornately carved feet, opened the decorative door and lifted the lid of a wooden safe box sitting on the shelf. He slipped her letter inside then returned to his chair. "Zenia tells me the warrior James MacDonald knows all. If you're to live here, then you'll have to cut your ties with him."

"Zenia explained your sister wed the Chief of MacLean and the MacLeans and MacDonalds are at war."

"'Tis a deadly feud that rages between them." He scrubbed a hand over his thick brown beard speckled with gray. "And my sister's enemy is my enemy. I cannae associate with the MacDonalds, no' even one who has aided you."

"I don't wish to cause any problems."

"Good." He nodded. "Then 'tis settled. You are welcome in my home and you will be known as my late cousin's daughter from Skye. That should suffice."

"Will I be able to visit Zenia?"

"As often as you wish." He nodded at Zenia. "I find I am more than intrigued. All will be as you've asked."

"My thanks." Relief poured through her. Arianna would be

well cared for and that was all she could ever ask.

* * * *

Back at her cottage, Zenia and Arianna rejoined James as he paced her front room in a white tunic and tan trews, his daggers sheathed at each wrist and his sword belted at his side. The warrior raised one eyebrow. "What did the earl say, Zenia?"

"He—"

"He said yes." Arianna squealed and jumped into James's arms. The two had formed a close bond over the weeks she'd been confined to her bed. She doubted Arianna would be able to cut all ties with James. 'Twould be an impossibility. "I'm to pack my things and return immediately and I'm allowed to visit Zenia as often as I wish," Arianna told him. "There is only one stipulation I didn't care for."

"And what is that?"

"I'm not allowed to see you. So that means whenever you visit, you'll need to do so in secret."

"Aye, that I can manage." He grinned then slowly frowned. "I came across William again this morn and we fought. I explained to him I gave you my word of protection and that will always stand firm, whether he wishes it or no'." He gestured toward his leather satchel on the tabletop underneath the window. "I bought a gift for you. I wanted you to have it afore I left."

"Is it one of those sugared plums you returned with after your last trip to the village? Those were delicious." She scooped his satchel up and passed it to him.

"Nay, you look inside." He handed the satchel back to her, sat on the wooden bench and patted the space beside him. "Now you'll be out and about, you must take every precaution and this gift will aid you in doing so."

She perched, opened the flap and peered inside. Slowly, reverently, she lifted a tiny wrapped package from within and opened it. She unwrapped the paper and plucked a silver disk free. "Oh, how beautiful. It's a charm."

"Turn it over and read the inscription." James tucked a lock of her blond hair behind her ear.

Arianna did and Zenia leaned forward and smiled as she read the words etched upon it.

Arianna MacLeod Cunningham
DOB: 1569.

"It's perfect and you're so thoughtful." Arianna touched her heart. "I love it." She passed the charm to James. "Can you put it on for me?"

"Of course." He unfastened her necklace, removed the old charm and added the new. "I can look after your old charm if you wish."

"Only if you promise to keep it safe."

"I'll guard it with my life. That I promise you, just as I gave you my word I shall always be here for you." He brought her hands to his lips, kissed her knuckles and stood. "Now, I must be away afore the day is done."

"I hate that you have to leave." She hugged him. "Travel safely and hurry back. I'll be waiting."

"I'll return as often as my duties allow it." He stroked the back of her head and closed his eyes.

The two had formed an unbreakable bond, just as Zenia and Arianna had done. Together, she and James would continue to guard her, their little imp who'd traveled through time.

Chapter 1

Four years later, on the way to Dunvegan Castle, stronghold of clan MacLeod, Isle of Skye, 1590.

Arianna's heartbeat raced as she sat in a birlinn in the dark of night surrounded by the earl, Zenia, and a good twenty of their Cunningham warriors as they sailed along the final seaward stretch toward Dunvegan Castle to join in this year's Highland Games being held on Skye. She longed to experience the week of festivities where the clans gathered and challenged each other, but even more so, to once again be back on land so close to her childhood home.

Overhead, a thick layer of cloud parted and moonlight shimmered through and cast a silvery hue over the forest's treetops edging the coastline. So beautiful. "I've missed this place."

"As have I." Zenia jiggled on the wooden bench seat. "'Tis been twenty-one long years since I was last here. I left no' long after my mother's passing and never returned."

"I'm so glad we've come together." Arianna had begged the earl to allow her to journey here even though his wife was unable to. She'd asked if Zenia could chaperone her and when he'd said yes, she couldn't have been more thrilled. Leaning closer to Zenia, she asked, "Why have you stayed away for so long?"

"I shouldnae have, but I experienced so much loss those last few months I was here. I lived at the castle and my mother was the old chief's healer afore her passing." She lowered her voice further. "Have I ever told you how Cunningham's father, the old earl, came to meet my mother?"

"Only that they met here." Zenia had told her what she'd told no other, the truth of who her father was. Even Cunningham was unaware. All he knew was that Zenia's father had been from his clan.

"The old earl visited his kinsmen here from time to time and when he did he stayed at Dunvegan. 'Twas on one such visit he met my mother and at a time when she was rather young and impressionable."

"That's when they had their affair?"

"Aye, and when it was time for the earl to leave, my mother discovered she was with child and spoke of it to him. She believed herself in love with him, but of course the old earl had no intention of leaving his wife." With a slight tip of her head, she motioned toward the earl as he stood and strode to the center mast and gripped it. "The old earl's son must never know."

"In the future, children are often born out of wedlock and there is no shame."

"Aye, but this isnae the future." With a gentle smile, she snuggled deeper into her red and blue tartan blanket. "Tell me all about Dunvegan Castle as you knew it. I adore hearing you speak of the future."

"I have so many wonderful memories of this place. Dad used to purchase seasonal tickets and brought me here often. I used to listen in on the tours and can likely recite a ton of its history, but there's one secret I must tell you that no one can know."

"What is it?"

"In the mid seventeen-hundreds, the current Chief of MacLeod did something no one ever believed would be possible. He built a landward entrance into Dunvegan."

"Nay." She gasped and sat upright. "But Dunvegan is built on a rock and the loch surrounds most of it. 'Tis inaccessible to reach by land. Surely you jest."

"I promise I'm speaking the truth. There's even a secret tunnel deep underneath the castle that weaves all the way to the land. I haven't been inside it, but it's there and I know it exists."

"A tunnel as well? Oh my." Awe shone in her blue eyes. "What else can you share? What of the MacLeod Fairy Flag? Quite by chance, my mother saw it as a child. Usually 'tis kept well hidden by the chief."

The Fairy Flag was one of their MacLeod clan's most treasured possessions. Decades ago, the fairy princess had fallen in love with the MacLeod chief and begged her father, the fairy king, to allow them to wed. He'd told her she would tire of the human world and wish to return to their people. When she'd declared she wouldn't and once again pleaded, her father instead made her an offer. She could handfast with the MacLeod chief but after a year and a day had passed, she must return to the fairy realm. She and the chief wed and she bore him a son, and when the time came for her to honor her word and return to her people, she asked her handfast husband to promise her that he'd never allow their son to be left alone for if she ever heard him cry, it would tear her heart in two. The chief kept his word and ensured a nursemaid watched over their son at all times, but one day the maid lapsed in her duties and when the princess heard her son's cries, she rushed to him and comforted him then wrapped him in her shawl. When the nursemaid returned, she found the child sleeping peacefully, swathed in a beautiful crimson and yellow patterned cloth. A cloth known from that moment on as the Fairy Flag.

"In the future," Arianna whispered, "the Fairy Flag no

longer remains hidden. It actually sits within a frame in the great hall for all to see, although it's merely a wispy scrap of fabric. Still, I've stood before it and it possesses such an ethereal beauty. Your mother must have been one of the few to have laid eyes on it in this time."

"She was." Zenia breathed deep and sighed as a sad look crossed her face. "I miss her, so much, and Samuel. This return trip to Dunvegan has brought back some poignant memories." Zenia spoke from time to time of Samuel Cunningham, the man she'd been betrothed to. She'd loved him dearly and had never bound herself to another man since. She couldn't, not when Samuel still held her heart.

"Where did your Samuel live?"

"Near the village with his brother until he came of age. Then he moved into the barracks at Dunvegan and trained with my MacLeod kin. Before too long he became one of the old chief's captains. He was a strong and a fierce fighter. 'Twas no' long after we celebrated our betrothal that war broke out on the neighboring Isle of Lewis and Tormod offered our Lewis kin his aid. Both Samuel and my mother sailed to their shores."

"I'm so sorry you lost both of them the way you did. I don't know quite how you dealt with it all."

"Those were some of my darkest days. Tormod told me Mother's death was fast, and Samuel's injury was so severe his breath rattled in and out as he hovered at the edge of death. Tormod did all he could and sent my beloved soaring free, body and soul. The old chief held the same skill as I." She stared out over the blackened waves then wiped a trickling tear from her cheek. "'Twas hard no' having Samuel's body to bury, although Tormod returned with my mother's, her soul at ease."

"Dunvegan lies directly ahead," Cunningham called.

"Oh, we're almost there." Zenia lifted a little to get a better view and Arianna followed suit.

Ahead, Dunvegan rose from the dark like a fortress, its

massive gray towers and fortified walls topped with battlements and guardsmen roaming the ramparts. From the multitude of square windows, candlelight flickered in welcome. Such a glorious sight. "I can't believe I'm about to meet Rory MacLeod. He's known as one of the greatest chiefs of our clan."

"Rory's been to Glencairn over the years, but no' while you've lived there."

"Lower the sail!" Cunningham stood in his great plaid and thick black boots, looking as eager as them all to make landfall. "All to oars."

The warriors plunged their oars into the depths, speeding their birlinn toward the sea-gate. At the edge of the stone landing, two large men waded into the water and as they came abreast of them, each seized a side of the birlinn. Hearty welcomes rang out from the two warriors as they guided the birlinn the last few feet and nestled it next to the stone stairs.

Another warrior walked along the landing toward them, his green eyes glinting with specks of yellow from the flickering torch he held. He offered Arianna his hand. "Watch your step, my lady. The rocks are slippery."

"Thank you." She grasped ahold and he aided her out. Her legs shook from being confined to one position for so long but she stamped her feet and wriggled her toes as they tingled anew.

The earl bounded out onto the landing and eyed the warrior. "We're here at the Chief of MacLeod's invitation. Could you please ensure he's made aware of our—"

"Well, well, if it isnae Cunningham." A towering man descended the stone stairs. Leather trews hugged his thick legs and a buckskin vest molded his broad chest. His dark blond hair, tied back with a strip of leather, gave him a formidable look, as did the battle-axe and sword holstered at his hip. Their Viking heritage couldn't have been more obvious.

"Rory MacLeod." Cunningham stepped up to him. "'Tis good to see you again."

"Welcome to Dunvegan. You and your kin are only the second of the competing clans to arrive. The remainder are due to sail in on the morrow. I've had chambers prepared for you and your kin and pallets laid down in the barracks for your men."

"My thanks." He motioned toward William as he joined them. "William, you've met Rory."

"I have, though 'tis been a while." William adjusted his bow and arrow satchel over one shoulder and shook Rory's hand. At twenty-four, William stood tall, almost eye to eye with Rory.

"Welcome, William. I see my warriors will have some healthy competition during these Games."

"I'm looking forward to the sword challenge in particular."

"Aye, as am I." Rory grinned as Zenia stood and walked to the side of the boat. He offered her a steadying hand as she stepped onto the landing in her blue gown and cloak, her tartan blanket tucked over one arm. "My favorite healer. 'Tis been far too long since you last set foot on Skye, Zenia."

"'Tis wonderful to be home again." Her cheeks flushed a rosy hue. "I hope you'll take care while I'm here no' to climb any trees."

He chuckled. "I shall never live my tree climbing days down with you. How many broken bones of mine did you mend when I was a lad?"

"Far more than I should have, although because of you I did learn how to mend a limb very well."

"That you did."

Cunningham gestured toward Arianna. "Rory, allow me to introduce you to Arianna MacLeod Cunningham. Her late father was a close cousin of mine. Like Zenia, she too has a great love of healing and intends to offer her aid where she can during these Games."

"Another MacLeod. 'Tis good to meet you. Do your kin come from Skye?"

"Yes. I used to live not far from here along the inner channel of the loch toward Dunvegan Village." She dipped her head. "I'm so excited to be here."

"Then come. You must meet my sister, Margaret. She longs for female company. Allow me to lead the way." He strode along the rocky path winding upward, lit by the odd torch staked into the stony ground.

Once they reached the top, they tramped through a darkened passageway and into an inner courtyard. Torches mounted on the stone walls spread their flickering glow while above on the battlements, guardsmen patrolled the ramparts in battle attire and weapons holstered at their sides.

Ahead, the stone entry of the keep beckoned. A boisterous buzz of voices echoed toward her and she took a deep, fortifying breath and entered the great hall. The vaulted room held high wooden beamed rafters, and the plastered walls were covered with beautiful tapestries, of hunting and landscape scenes. Trestle tables were stacked with large platters of cooked meat, roasted vegetables, and bread, while a good hundred warriors in their MacLeod tartan sat on wooden benches enjoying the fine looking fare. Serving maids carried trays holding steaming bowls of stew and bustled about. Never had she seen the castle so alive like this. Hand to her mouth, she turned in a circle, embracing it all. Her father would have loved to have witnessed this. Countless times they'd stood together in this hall then wandered through the public rooms. Her vision blurred and she pushed back threatening tears. Being here again was a dream come true even though it stirred such bittersweet memories.

"I cannae believe we must sit in the same hall as the MacDonalds." William snorted as he gripped his bow.

At the far trestle table, a score of warriors wore the distinctive red, blue and green tartan of the MacDonald clan. She searched amongst the warriors and gasped as one of them rose to his feet. James's great plaid was secured over his chest with a silver pin and belted low at his waist with a leather girdle. His vivid blue gaze, as deep as the ocean, settled on her and her heartbeat fluttered. She hadn't seen him in six agonizing long months, not since his chief had been captured and imprisoned by the king and tossed into Holyrood's tower. He appeared taller, stronger, and his thick biceps bulged as he slid one thumb under his claymore's front belted strap. The hilt of the mighty sword strapped in a baldric across his back gleamed under the candlelit chandelier above.

"Arianna." William's tone was stern as he squeezed her shoulder. "Avert your gaze. Dinnae draw James MacDonald's attention."

"I haven't seen him in so long." Even though she'd tried to meet with James in secret during those times he'd visited, William more often than not learnt of his arrival and the two usually fought. Not once had she been able to stop them.

"He's the enemy and a man you need to steer well clear of." He clenched his teeth.

"He's also one of my guardians whether you wish it or not. Rescuing me from James isn't necessary."

William stroked one finger smoothly down the length of his bow's string line. "Father recently received word from one of my aunt's men that James has not long been at Holyrood House. Apparently he was there to court Rory's cousin, Annie MacLeod. Clearly he seeks an alliance although under the guise of wishing for peace between the clans."

"He intends to wed?" She and James kept nothing from each other. He would have said. "Are you sure?"

"His brother recently spoke vows with another of Rory's close kin. The signs of his clan's intentions are all there." He jerked his head toward the dais where an elegant young lady sat in a corseted cream gown, her pale hair curling in long locks down her back. The fine velvet hugged her trim waist, the gold and red silk ribbons lacing the front an entwining of rich colors.

"That's Rory's sister, Margaret, and now she's eight and ten, I would lay a wager James will be after a contract with her, either by marriage or handfast."

"She's barely of age."

"Women may wed far younger than that. Come." William set a hand at her back and steered her across the room after Rory toward the dais.

The MacLeod chief smiled at his sister. "Margaret, you'll remember the Earl of Glencairn and his son, William."

"I do." Her eyes twinkled as she smiled at them both.

"The earl has also brought his ward, Arianna, and the healer, Zenia MacLeod, as her chaperone. Look after the ladies for me and ensure they know where their chambers are."

"Certainly." Margaret patted the chairs either side of her as Rory offered a seat to Cunningham and William farther along the table. "Come and join me. There are so few women here and I long for female company."

"Thank you." Arianna sat, arranged her sapphire skirts around her and accepted a bowl of stew the serving maid offered her.

Margaret picked up the large pitcher and filled two goblets with warm cider and passed one to her and the other to Zenia. "I've heard so many wonderful tales about you, Zenia, and your late mother. 'Tis intriguing to finally meet you."

"There is little intriguing about me."

"Oh, but I've heard you hold the gifted skill, the same as what my father did." Margaret leaned closer to Zenia as she whispered, "Is that no' the truth?"

"Aye, 'tis the truth. Tormod first taught me all I needed to know about my ability. He was a fine chief and I admired him so." Zenia picked up her spoon and ate a mouthful. "Mmm, this is delicious."

Arianna closed her eyes and breathed in the mouth-watering scent of mutton and vegetables. They'd been traveling for close to a week, eating dried foods and oatcakes. Hot meals had been few and far between and now her belly rumbled. She scooped up the wedge of bread at the side, took a big bite and licked the richly flavored juices as they dribbled from the end. Hearty and delicious.

Margaret selected a morsel of salmon from her trencher and chewed. "I've never traveled as far south as Glencairn. What is the land like there, Arianna?"

"As wild and as beautiful as these isles, although missing the sea since we're some distance inland. It's been an age since I've sailed these waterways."

"Rory has promised to take me to Holyrood House on his next trip this coming spring, although I believe we'll be traveling by road most of the way." She grinned and looked out over the feasting warriors. "It's wonderful to see the clans coming together like this. I so enjoy the Games."

Warriors clanked their tankards together and drank. Food and drink flowed and James nodded at her from his seat next to his men. She smiled and touched her heart. He was so close, yet still so far away, although regardless of William's warning, she would speak to James.

Nothing and no one would stop her.

* * * *

The Cunningham clan had arrived except James had not expected Arianna to be among them. A healthy glow flushed her cheeks and he longed to trace the smattering of sweet freckles across her nose. Six long months had passed since he'd last seen her and he'd never have allowed so much time to pass if it weren't for his clan's feuding with the MacLean of Duart, or his chief's capture by the king's men. He and his brother had fought hard to protect Dunscaith Castle and their lands, but this trip to Dunvegan to participate in the Games had been a necessity, just as his recent trip to Edinburgh to visit his imprisoned chief in the king's tower had been. Donald MacDonald had made his request to him clear. He was to strengthen the ties between the MacDonalds and the MacLeods so the MacLeans would not have such a strong ally against them in this war. If possible, he was to woo Rory's sister, and since it was peace James sought, in many ways he agreed with his chief's plan.

"William Cunningham watches you. So does the earl." Artair, his right hand man, clapped him on the shoulder. "Is there a reason you've already drawn their attention?"

"Possibly." At the dais, Arianna stood, her long golden blond tresses shimmering in the firelight. She eased back into the shadows then disappeared down a darkened hallway. He nodded at Artair and said, "Keep your eye on William and ensure he does no' follow me. I have a wee errand to run."

"Aye, Captain."

He slipped behind a screened doorway and weaved his way around the back passageway toward the hallway Arianna had taken. The gloomy corridor, lit only by the odd candle in an iron wall sconce, remained bare of any other. He slowed near a darkened alcove opposite a half-opened paneled door. This antechamber was one the men used at night when they wished to play a game of cards or converse in private. He'd been in here earlier this eve. With one hand on his sword hilt, he gently, carefully, prodded the door open. It swung wide and Arianna stood in the moonlight beaming through the narrow window. He stepped inside and closed the door. "What are you doing here?" he rasped.

"And hello to you too." Smiling, she set a lit candle in a holder on top of the center table surrounded by six lavishly upholstered chairs.

"There is danger in this meeting."

"There's always danger when you and I meet." She stepped closer and with a soft sigh, pressed her palm against his chest.

Heat radiated from her touch and his fingers twitched with the need to pull her into his arms. He wanted to hold her, as badly as he always did. Instead he shoved his hands behind his back. He was here for peace, which meant forming an alliance with the MacLeods.

Slowly, he stepped back then wandered around the chamber with its bright yellow plastered walls. At the far side, he sat where he could easily watch the door and her.

"Please, I don't like to see you so worried." She crossed to him, her full velvet skirts brushing the polished floorboards. She looked a vision, her gown's square-cut neckline dipping and exposing the swell of her creamy skin. "William told me tonight you might have your sights set on Margaret MacLeod. Is that true?"

"William needs to mind his own business."

"She's only eighteen."

"I'm well aware."

"You intend to offer for her?" She dipped a finger below the embroidered edging of her bodice and freed her silver necklace. She clasped the charm he'd given her firmly in her palm.

"There's a strong possibility, although I've only spoken to her once and that was earlier this eve on my arrival." He eased back in his chair. "My clan's feud with the MacLeans has escalated. My last trip to Edinburgh was to visit my captured chief. I desire peace, Arianna. This war between the clans must come to an end and if an alliance must be made between myself and Margaret, then so be it." He dug into his pocket and gripped her charm, the one he'd promised he'd always keep safe, one he always kept on him.

"I understand your need for peace, but I've missed you."

"As I've missed you." He pressed his elbows to the table. Arianna had made her position clear time and time again. She longed to save her ill father and return to the future, however that could be achieved. There was no place in her life for him. "Does Cunningham still treat you well?"

"Yes. The earl is good to me." She fidgeted with her sapphire gown's long sleeves, tugging the lace hem that draped over her knuckles.

"Then what concerns you? Your agitation is obvious. Speak as you will. You've never held aught back from me afore."

"It's been four years and I'm still here. I'm no closer to returning home than I was at the very beginning."

"Zenia can only call forth her ability if there is a lost soul in need of it."

"I am a lost soul." She swished to his side, hand thumping her chest. "My father is all I have other than you and Zenia, and if you wed another, I'll be forced to let you go too."

"I will always be here for you." Her anguish tore at him and he stood, caught her hand and tugged her closer. Hell, he'd never been able to resist her. "If you've changed your mind and wish to stay in the past, then say the word and I'll pursue you instead." He would, in an instant.

"This isn't my time and it never will be." She leaned her forehead against his chest. "My father needs me."

"I would care for you as none other could."

"I know you would, but I have to halt his death before it happens." She lifted her chin, tears pooling in her eyes. "The disease that takes him can be averted, provided I can get word to him before it does. His life is worth everything to me, and now I'm back on Skye, there must be something more I can do." A lone tear streaked down her cheek and he wiped it away.

"Dinnae cry."

"I feel so torn. I just learnt you're considering another and it hurts."

"We are in a predicament then." He wrapped his arms around her and gently stroked her back. "The feud worsens," he murmured.

"How bad is it?"

"Lachlan MacLean recently attacked my chief's brother and

his clan on the Isle of Islay. He attempted to burn the village of Ardbeg to the ground and when unsuccessful, captured the MacDonald chief's wife and his eldest son. Lachlan MacLean then took to the Rhinns on Islay's western coast and when the MacDonalds of Islay caught up with him, a battle ensued. MacLean was captured and handed over to the king's men, although the MacLeans now seek their revenge against our fellow clansmen. Which means we too must be prepared. Another attack could come at any time."

"I understand your duty is to your clan." She caught his hand, opened his fist and smiled as she gazed at her old charm.

Hell, if he lowered his head, he could claim her lips and the kiss he'd always longed for.

"In the future, one usually marries for love." She traced one finger along his lower lip.

"You must no' touch me so, no' unless you wish for more."

"What I wish for is to have both you and my father, but that will never—" She glanced at the door.

Footsteps echoed down the passageway and swiftly, he tucked Arianna in behind him and clasped his sword. "It appears we're about to have company. Do you wish to take one guess who that might be?"

She sighed. "As much as I adore him, William is like a hound, always scenting his prey. I should leave before he—"

William opened the door and entered, his gaze narrowing on James. "Why am I no' surprised to find you once again meeting in an inappropriate place and time with Arianna?"

"You cannae deny me my duty, and as one of her guardians, I'll meet with her as often as I wish."

"As you always say, and as I always disagree." William bounded forward, sword raised.

* * * *

"No. You two need to stop this." Arianna dived between William and James as they came at each other. Breathing hard, she shoved one hand against each of their chests. "I'm sick of watching you two fight."

"Step aside, Arianna." William's face turned thunderously dark.

"You can't scare me with that look of yours. Honestly, you two are both on the same side when it comes to protecting me. I wish you'd see that."

"You've no need of a MacDonald. His clan are at war with my aunt's MacLean kin. He would gladly take the life of any one of them."

"Only if provoked." James glared at William. "Lower your weapon and I shall do the same. It isnae right to bring Arianna into our disagreement."

William slid his sword away as he eyed her. "I warned you. You're to stay away from him, yet at the first opportunity you defy me."

"You might be at war with James but I'm not, and I have a request to make of him, a very important one which was why I had to see him."

"You can make any request you have need of directly to me."

"Nay, she sought me out, William." James sheathed his blade and crossed his arms. "Speak as you will, Arianna."

"Now I'm back on Skye"—she remained firmly between them—"I'd like to visit my father's home on the land where his ancestors lived, and I'd like you to take me."

"What are your intentions if I allow this?"

"To leave a letter with them, one they can pass along. I've got to do something more to save my father. I fear the reason I'm still here in the past is because none of my letters have yet reached him. Maybe once one does, I'll no longer be a lost soul."

William scoffed. "Father's safe overflows with your letters. One will surely reach him."

James set a hand on her shoulder. "If you wish to deliver

another letter to your father, I'll gladly aid you, but there will be conditions. Although give me some time to consider them all, then we'll speak again."

"Of course. Whatever you ask I'll gladly agree to."

"Good." He strode to the door and glanced over his shoulder at her. "I'll see you on the morrow. Take care this eve."

"I will. Thank you." Excitement bubbled inside her. James never backed down on a promise. She would get her wish, to leave her father another letter. Nothing could have made her happier.

Chapter 2

With William at her side, Arianna walked from the room and along the gloomy passageway lit by the odd flickering candle in its iron wall sconce.

"No more secret assignations with MacDonald," William warned in a low growl.

"James wishes to form an alliance with the MacLeods, but to ensure peace between the clans, not for the reason you spoke of earlier. I really wish you two would get along."

"I'm sure that's exactly what James told you." His tone said he would never fall such a thing.

"Even though I adore you, you're impossible sometimes." Ahead in the great hall, the pipers played a merry tune and she left William and strode back to her seat.

"I'm so sorry, my dear. I couldnae stop William from seeking you out. One of James's men tried to divert him too but to no avail." Zenia shuffled closer, taking Margaret's vacated chair. The chief's sister twirled around the dance floor where the trestle tables had been moved to make more room. The young woman looped her arm through another warrior's, her cream skirts flying and her giggles floating free. The chief's sister was gracious, bright and bubbly. She'd make a wonderful wife for any man.

"At least this time they didn't actually draw blood." She drummed her fingers on the tabletop.

"Excuse me, my ladies." One of their clansmen, a seasoned warrior who Zenia had healed from a nasty arm wound only a month ago, dipped his head toward his now favorite healer. "Would ye care for a birl?"

"Oh, I'd love that." Zenia squeezed her hand as she stood. "Cheer up, my dear, and try to enjoy yourself."

"Don't worry about me. You go and have some fun for the both of us."

"Oh, I surely will." She took the hulking warrior's elbow and he spun her away.

Across the hall, James reappeared from behind a screened door and sat with his kinsmen while Margaret danced back to her seat and flopped into her chair. "I see your brother found you. He appeared worried about where you'd gotten to."

"Brothers are extremely annoying."

She laughed. "Oh, you're speaking to the converted. Two brothers, and both so overbearing, I can barely walk about the courtyard without them snarling at any man who might wish to talk to me. I'm surprised I got one full dance in." Margaret grinned and nudged her shoulder with hers. "I couldnae help but notice the MacDonald captain watching you so intently."

"James is one of my guardians, not that William has ever approved."

"A guardian? Hmm, now that sounds interesting. How did that come about? The MacDonalds and Cunninghams have rarely seen eye to eye over the years. For you to have a MacDonald as a guardian is rather unusual."

"Not long after I lost my father, and before I entered the earl's household, James aided me when I was lost and alone. I'd suffered a terrible injury and along with Zenia, the two of them cared for me. Since that time, his protection has stood strong."

"My, my." Margaret patted her chest. "Then James is a man of great honor."

"Every single inch of him."

Across the hall, James glanced between her and Margaret, a frown on his face. Perhaps it would be best if she gave James the chance to speak to Margaret and get to know her as he likely wished to. Certainly with her here, doing so would be harder for him. His loyalty to her would stir, as well as his need not to hurt her.

She stood and smiled at Margaret. "I've been up since dawn and I'm exhausted. Would it be possible for you to show me to my chamber?"

"Aye. I should really have considered such a thing. Come." Margaret rose and led her toward the stairwell. She slowed as a maid walked toward her. "Bessie, have our guests' trunks been placed in their chambers?"

"Aye, my lady. Mistress Arianna's have been left in the gold chamber and Mistress Zenia's in the blue."

"Wonderful. Ensure both their fires are lit." Margaret walked up the curved stairs to the second floor and Arianna followed. Before one of the wall sconces, she removed a candle then opened a chamber door and set it in a holder by the bedside table. "Bessie willnae be long."

"Thank you. This room is beautiful." The chamber held a queen-sized bed with a thick golden canopy drawn around the sides. The rich velvet swept onto the polished wooden floors. "Is your chamber nearby?"

"I'm afraid no'. My chamber is in the Fairy Tower across the keep. Rory has his rooms there too."

Bessie knocked on the open door and hurried in. She knelt in her brown kirtle before the hearth and set to work building a fire.

"I'll say goodnight." Margaret squeezed her hands. "If there is aught more you need, then just ask."

"I will."

"I'll see you in the morn." With a smile, Margaret swished out the door and closed it behind her. Yes, she'd make a fine wife for any man. She was so considerate and caring.

The maid dusted her hands against her aproned sides and stood. The fire blazed and spread its delicious warmth throughout the room. "Would you like help readying yourself for bed, my lady?"

"I would. This gown laces at the back." She turned and Bessie loosened the laces. She wriggled the fabric over her hips and down her legs while the maid foraged through her trunk under the narrow window and returned with her nightrail. She eased the white linen shift she passed her over her head.

Bessie gathered the gown pooled on the floor and draped it over her arm. "I'll return this after it's been laundered, my lady."

"Thank you."

"Rest well." Bessie left and she closed and bolted the door behind the maid, crawled under the covers and snuggled. The blood feuds raging across the isles impacted all of Scotland and James's desire for peace was one she couldn't fault him for. If only this truly was her time. She would choose him in a heartbeat and never look back.

* * * *

As the entertainment drew to a close with the late hour, James strode upstairs toward his chamber on the second floor, his satchel and weapons in hand. His men had been offered pallets in the barracks and he'd considered bedding down with them, but with Arianna's arrival, things had changed, particularly with her need to leave a letter with her Cunningham ancestors. There was danger in allowing too many to know the truth about where she'd came from. He'd certainly aid her in her mission to get a letter to her father, but above all else, he'd ensure she never exposed herself in the process.

Outside his chamber door, he stopped as his right hand man

slid out of the shadowed nook. With William keeping such a close eye on him, he'd asked his man to follow Arianna when she'd retired for the night and ensure she remained safe. "Is her chamber close?" he asked Artair.

"Aye, she has the room next to yours, the one on the right. All remains quiet on this floor."

An edgy frustration sizzled through him, in part because his conversation with her remained unfinished and also because of the emotions that always reared to life when he was near her. "My thanks."

"I'll see you in the morn." Artair disappeared into the dark.

The Games were to begin in the afternoon once the remainder of the clans arrived, and as much as he enjoyed the gathering when hostilities between them all were set aside, 'twas only a momentary truce. He and his men would need to remain on guard, because no matter that he wished for peace, unless all the feuding clans did too, then he fought a losing battle.

He opened his door and stepped inside his room. Moonlight streamed through the narrow window and played over the thick brown fur covering his bed. He set his bag on the side table then propped his bow and satchel of arrows in the corner. He'd warm the chamber then seek out Arianna. Even though the hour was late, they needed to speak.

On his knees at the hearth, he tore bark from a log, struck his flint against his dagger and blew on the sparks. Flames flickered and he tossed a block of peat onto the fire. Behind him, a draught from somewhere rippled the ambry's navy curtains. The windows and door remained firmly shut. No wind had come down the chimney. He crossed to the ambry and pushed the curtain aside. A paneled door, lower and not as wide as most in the castle, was visible next to the shelves. He stroked the polished wood. This connecting door must lead directly into Arianna's chamber. The wall it stood against was to the right.

He slid the bolt free and without a snick of noise pushed the door open. Soundlessly, he stepped through. Golden drapery hid his path and he swished the curtain back.

Arianna slept in a large four-poster bed, her pale blond lashes glimmering in the fire's glow. She was such an innocent.

He knelt at her side and smoothed his knuckles across her soft cheeks. Everything about her touched him, from her absolute devotion to those she loved to her feisty and fierce nature. He breathed deep and her sweet vanilla scent swirled seductively around him. From the moment he'd carried her into Zenia's cottage and she'd burrowed against him, he'd experienced an overwhelming sense of rightness, one that had grown over the years from strength to strength. Being with her, holding her, was all he desired. Hell, how on earth was he meant to court another woman when she was the one he wanted?

During his recent trip to see his chief in the king's cells, he'd actually attempted to court Rory's cousin, Annie MacLeod, while at Holyrood. When Annie had instead handfasted with Colin MacLean, relief had poured through him. Even though the MacLean warrior was his adversary, he couldn't begrudge either of them their desired union. If only Arianna wished for what he did, but in the four years since her arrival she'd never once changed her course of mind. Her aspiration was to return to her father, a dream he couldn't and wouldn't deny her.

"Mmm, James." Arianna pushed her arms out from under the covers, dislodging the tartan blanket. Her nightrail remained loose at the top, the ties partially undone and exposing the upper swell of her breasts. "Don't leave me, James. You promised should I ever have need of you, you'd come," she murmured in her sleep.

"I'm here." He hauled the blanket back up to her neck. Her lush creamy skin would send him insane if he saw any more of it.

"James?" She blinked her eyes open and sat up, the dratted tartan slipping to her waist. "How did you get in here?" She searched the room. "The door's bolted."

"We have adjoining chambers and there's a connecting door inside your ambry that leads to mine. Your, ah"—he motioned toward her chest—"nightrail is loose."

"Oh." She yanked the ties together and closed the gap. "What a stroke of good luck to have adjoining rooms."

"William wouldnae think so."

"Then we'd best not tell him." Smiling, she wriggled across and patted the mattress. "Sit with me. Now we finally have a decent chance to talk."

"Aye, we do." He toed off his boots, propped his sword beside her bed where it would lay within easy reach and sat beside her. They'd talk, and then he'd leave. She was a craving he had to set aside, for both their sakes.

"You have a rather serious expression on your face." She plumped her pillow and propped it behind her.

"'Tis naught. I said we'd speak about your desire to seek out your Cunningham ancestors and the conditions you'll need to agree to when I take you. I willnae allow you to speak to them, to divulge your secret to another, but if you know of a safe place to keep your letter where your father might find it then I'll gladly aid you."

"I'm sure I can come up with somewhere." She popped a kiss on his cheek. "Thank you. I'm very grateful for all you do for me."

"You shouldnae kiss me." He palmed the place where the heat of her kiss still lingered.

"That wasn't a kiss." She leaned in again and this time licked his lower lip. "Neither was that, but I'm getting closer."

Desire surged through his blood and he growled her name, gripped her arms and pressed her back into the mattress with his body. Looming over her, he hoped like hell he had a stern enough expression on his face. "This is your last warning. You shouldnae kiss me."

"You seem rather bent out of shape over what I wouldn't even call a kiss." She wriggled her body and her nipples poked her thin nightrail. "Honestly, I'd like to kiss you. It might help me stop wondering what it might be like."

"You need to watch your words as well." His cock hardened and pressed into her belly. "Do you no' feel what you do to me? I want you Arianna. I always have."

"Then kiss me. We're alone and no one can interrupt us." She slid her hands free of his hold, wrapped her arms around his neck then gently, drew him closer. "One kiss, and we'll make it count."

"Arianna, from the day you arrived you've held a piece of my heart and you always will. I long to be with you. I only fear I'll never be able to give you up if I allow my feelings such a release."

"And I fear returning to the future and having never known your touch. Which means we're at a stalemate, although it's one I still intend to win." She smiled and his resolve fluttered away. "James, let's forget about what could or couldn't be and just live in the moment. You and me. There's no one else here but us. One kiss." She threaded her fingers deep into his hair, guided his mouth to hers and kissed him. Her breath whispered softly across his tongue, a teasing caress that made his blood roar in his ears.

He urged her lips apart to capture more of her essence and lost himself. She tasted divine, so sweetly pure yet with an edge of hunger that matched his own. Need rushed through him and he took control of their kiss, plunged his tongue inside her mouth and drank in her delectable innocence. He welcomed the raw intimacy, one he'd craved for so long. Damn, he was losing control. He pulled back, only an inch, but hopefully enough to restore some much needed sanity.

"Maybe two kisses might be best." She pressed her breasts against his chest, kissed his jaw and nibbled toward his ear. "I feel hot, very hot."

"Then I should leave."

"No, stay." She caressed his sides then roamed down over his rear.

"This is dangerous. We both play with fire."

"I agree it's dangerous, but maybe necessary." She spread her hands wide and aligned their bodies completely. "I'm twenty-one and old enough to decide who I want in my bed, and since you're here and we're being honest with each other, that man is you."

"I willnae take your innocence. That right belongs to your husband and I didnae come in here to ravish you." He had to insert some space between them, to clear his head. He lifted himself from her and rolled to his side. "'Tis been a long day and we both need to rest."

"Well, I'm wide awake now."

"I'll stay until you fall asleep." Unable to leave her, he tucked her against his side and pulled the covers over them both. "Close your eyes."

"You are one stubborn man."

"Thank you."

"That wasn't a compliment." She shook her head but thankfully closed her eyes.

Time passed and slowly her breathing evened out.

The moment she succumbed to sleep, he closed his own eyes and allowed himself a few minutes' rest.

* * * *

A sliver of sunlight beamed through the wooden shutters over the narrow window and stirred James from his slumber. Arianna slept in his arms, her nose burrowed into his neck and her leg draped across his lower body. Her possessive hold on him had his groin tightening.

"James?" Mumbling, she stretched and sighed.

"Shh, go back to sleep." He shouldn't have stayed in her bed, but he'd needed to hold her, and before he no longer had the chance to do so.

Carefully, he extricated himself from her warmth, hauled on his boots and strapped on his sword belt. At the hearth, he prodded the embers back into blazing life and tossed a slab of peat on the fire to ensure she remained warm.

"Is it dawn already?" She propped herself up on her elbows, her pale hair a tangled mess around her shoulders as she blinked and opened her eyes.

"Aye, and the castle will soon awaken." He walked to her ambry and pushed the golden curtain aside. "I want you to be careful while you're here. Keep Zenia close. There are many warriors about."

"I promise I'll be careful. What events are you competing in?" She hopped out of bed and jumped onto his booted feet. "Sorry, but you move too fast and I had to stop you. Oh, look." She peered through the open door into his chamber then wobbled and slid her arms around his waist. "This will be a terrible temptation having you so close now I know how deliciously you kiss."

"I'll bar the door on my side." He couldn't keep the grumble from his voice. Locking her away from him was the last thing he wished to do.

"You can leave it unlocked. I won't mind at all." She smiled, so brightly he wanted to remain in her sight and soak the warmth of her gaze in. "Would it be too presumptuous of me to ask for a final kiss?"

"Very."

"What if I choose to offer one as a token of good luck for when you compete? I've heard holding a charm from a lady is very important." Challenge lit her stunning blue eyes.

"I already hold a charm of yours." Arms around her, he walked into his chamber with her clinging, her feet still atop his and her hips rocking snugly against his groin. How was he supposed to keep control when she teased and tempted him like this?

"I believe you could use another charm, two are far better than one alone." She ran her thumb along his lower lip then raised her gaze to his. "But of course that is your choice."

"There is no choice when it comes to you." He dipped his head, covered her mouth with his and kissed her with all the passion within him. His senses swam and he cupped her bottom, lifted her higher and made certain she felt every hard inch of him. "See how you tempt me?"

"Yes, and you do the same to me." She seized his biceps then kissed him back, until their breath mingled as one and the heat between them blazed.

Damn, he had to stop. Where was his resolve?

Breathing hard, he pulled away. "My thanks for your token of good luck."

"Anytime." She licked her lips.

Heaven help him. He was lost.

* * * *

Arianna spread her hand over James's solid chest. His muscles flexed under her touch and she embraced the heat that surged through her. He looked so rumpled and delicious with a razz of stubble on his jaw and his silky auburn hair catching the morning light and sparking like fire.

A muffled knock sounded, one not from his door but hers.

"You should go." James lifted her off his feet and onto the ground.

"I should." She forced herself to step back through the door into her room. He was everything she'd ever desired in a man. If only it was possible to be with him. Why couldn't she have it all, her father and him? "I'll talk to you later."

"Aye, later."

"Arianna?" Another knock. "'Tis Zenia. I ordered you a bath and the lads are here with the tub."

"Coming." Heart heavy, she closed the connecting door,

carefully rearranged the ambry curtain so it covered the entrance then crossed to her door. She greeted Zenia with a wide a smile. "Good morning."

"And a good morn to you too." Zenia swished inside in her bronze skirts, a color that highlighted her long red-gold curls. She moved to one side then bid the two lads behind her to enter.

Barefoot and with sooty marks on the knees of their loose-legged tan breeches, they heaved a tub before the fireplace then hurried out. A servant entered carrying a tray with two steaming bowls of oats and a trencher of sliced meats and placed it on the side table.

Another maid arrived, set a drying cloth and bar of soap next to the tub, while another lass crossed to her trunk and lifted the lid. With an armful of her clothing, she whooshed to the ambry and carefully hung each of the gowns in turn. The maid glanced at her. "What do you wish to wear, my lady?"

"The silvery-blue gown. Leave it on the bed if you could, please."

"Aye, I shall." She did then directed the lads as they returned with pails of steaming water. She added vanilla scented oil and a sprinkle of dried petals then done, closed the door behind her after the servants had filed out.

"Come and eat." Zenia ambled across to the side table and sat. Most mornings she walked the short distance to Zenia's cottage and they ate breakfast together. Such a special time, just the two of them before the day began.

"This looks delicious." She perched on the wooden backed chair, lifted the small bowl of honey and swirled it over top of hers and Zenia's hot oats. She slid a spoonful into her mouth. Delicious, and it tasted exactly like Dad made for her on those cold winter mornings when she'd been a child. Her chest throbbed and she blinked furiously, suddenly fighting tears. Her loss hit when she least expected it, even after all these years. Cancer. It was a horrible disease, and it had struck Dad hard and fast.

"What's wrong?" Zenia patted her hand, her brow furrowed.

"I miss him." She rubbed her chest. "Dad's been on my mind since I arrived. He loved coming here to Dunvegan. He'd stride along the battlements and watch the boats sailing out on the loch. Since he forged weapons of old, he had a huge fascination with the armory and its supply of arsenal."

"'Tis good for you to remember him."

"When I spoke to James last night, I asked him if he'd take me home. I'm going to write Dad another letter and ensure this one is stowed somewhere safe at the lodge." She gestured toward her ambry. "He and I have a connecting door, which is rather handy."

"Oh, this I must see." She rose, crossed the room and pushed the golden velvet and her newly hung gowns aside. "Well, I see I shall have to step up in my duties as chaperone."

"James told me last night he intends to court Margaret MacLeod. He said he seeks peace and hopes an alliance formed with Rory's sister will strengthen the ties between their clans."

"Such an alliance would be a wise move on James's behalf." She returned, sat and sipped her steaming tea.

"We kissed."

She arched a brow and set her tea down. "You are full of surprises this morn. James isnae the kind of man to kiss just any lass." She selected a bacon slice from the trencher and chewed.

"Saving my father is my priority."

"Of course Samuel Cunningham comes first."

"Why must so many marriages be made in order to strengthen clan ties?"

"'Tis the way of those of high standing. James is Donald MacDonald's nephew and his chief has never fathered any sons. From what I've seen James holds fast to his duty to his clan."

"I want more with James but not at the detriment of making

him give up his dream. Then there's also the issue that I'm not from this time and I have a dream of my own."

"I know, my dear. Your dream of returning to your father means the world to you. James would never stand in your way or ever deny you that." Zenia finished her breakfast then stood and knelt at the tub. She swirled her hand through the water. "This is the perfect heat. Come. Have your bath."

"I'm living in the past, yet no matter what I do, I can't bind myself to anyone here. There'd be too much pain when I left." She shed her nightrail and stepped into the bath. After sinking into the glorious water, she lazed her head on the rim and stroked the disk at her neck

"'Tis been four years and I believe you must live your life. One never knows how long we will have to walk this Earth." She knelt and lathered the soap. "I'll wash your hair. Dip down."

She slid under the water then emerged with a sigh. "James is beyond honorable, which is rather frustrating."

"So was my Samuel." Zenia worked the suds through her hair. "But I'm glad I managed to entice him to set that honorability aside, even if only for one night."

"You slept with Samuel?"

"Aye, I did, and our joining was a beautiful thing, although Samuel and I had promised ourselves to each other and we were to wed, something I must point out of course." Zenia motioned for her to go down. "The water cools and it's time to rinse."

She went down then came back up.

Zenia gently detangled her hair, separated it into sections then ran the comb through it. "I've spoken to Mattie, the healer here, and she's rather busy and lacking in supplies. I offered to do what I could to aid her so I agreed to collect herbs for her afore the Games begin this afternoon."

"Where do we collect them from?" With an elbow on the edge of the tub, she faced her.

"She recommended the forest bordering Dunvegan along

the coastline to the north. There is a stream between it and a grassy meadow, although without a landward gate, our only choice is to sail there. It isnae far. I could ask William to take us."

"Then I'd best hurry since he'll need to return before the sword challenge event begins. He's determined to topple the reigning champion." She hopped out of the water and dried herself. Quickly, she donned a shift then picked up the silvery-blue gown the maid had left and eased it over her head. The soft satin folds shimmered over her hips and swished to her ankles.

"There are few men who could topple Rory MacLeod. He's held the title of sword champion for the past three years. Allow me to lace the stays." Zenia did then turned her by the shoulders and pinched her cheeks. "Now you look all rosy. Let's be away."

She slid her matching slippers on and followed Zenia out the door. They traipsed down the winding stairs and entered the great hall abuzz with warriors attired in their clan plaids. The men sat at trestle tables stacked with platters of cooked meat, boiled eggs, and bread. They feasted and ate their fill.

"Do you see William?" Zenia collected two empty woven baskets from one of the side tables, looped one over her arm and passed the other to Arianna.

"No." She couldn't see any of her clansmen amongst the warriors. "He must have left for training with our men."

"Good morn, my ladies." James descended the stairs, his hair curling damply onto his shoulders. He'd bathed and looked completely edible in black leather trews and a white tunic under a fur vest. He eyed her basket. "Where are you off to this morn?"

"To collect a fresh supply of herbs. Dunvegan's healer requires more and Zenia offered our aid."

"Do you have an escort?"

"We were going to ask William but it appears he and our kin have left for training. We'll find a MacLeod guardsman to take us."

"Nay, I'll escort you to wherever you need to go. I'll be but one moment." He strode across the great hall and spoke to one of his warriors. The other man nodded and James nabbed a slice of bread from the trestle table, spread bacon rashes over it and a wedge of cheese then munched as he returned to them. "All is well. Where to, Zenia?"

"To the north, in the opposite direction to Dunvegan Village. There's a stream that borders a forest and a lush meadow. 'Tis the perfect place to find all we will need." She clasped her bronze skirts and walked toward the door.

"Are you certain you have the time to take us, James?" What of your training?"

"Training can wait, my imp." He tweaked her nose. "Your need of an escort is far greater." He extended an arm to her. "Allow me to offer my services. I willnae have just any guard watching over you."

"Then thank you." She slid her fingers through his crooked elbow and a buzz of awareness tingled her fingers and toes. She stroked his skin and curled her fingers around his arm. "I'll never say no to more time in your company."

"Neither shall I with you." He guided her outside and across the sundrenched inner courtyard as Zenia led the way. Under the tunnel's arch, they strolled and down the winding stony sea-gate path.

A seagull squawked as it flew overhead then dove into the rippling waves of the bay. It emerged with a fish and sprayed water as it heaved its wings and flew back into the air. "I've missed living by the sea. I hate the thought of leaving Skye at the end of the week."

"I would suffer greatly if I were forced to ever leave the isles. Those born here live and breathe the sea." He covered her hand with his. "I recently purchased a parcel of land that borders Dunscaith Castle along the coast. 'Tis bare of a residence, but once I have enough coin, I intend to build a castle. I shall make it my home."

"I'd love to see your land."

"I will show you one day. There's a private beach, one I discovered quite by chance while exploring the cliffs."

They joined Zenia where she'd halted on the landing ahead. Zenia hopped into his skiff nestled between two bobbing birlinns then sat on the wooden bench at the bow and set her basket under the seat.

James boarded, reached back for her and swung her in beside him.

Excitement bubbled through her as she settled at the rear near the rudder. "All to oars," she called then giggled. "I've always wanted to say that."

"You wish to captain my vessel?" James chuckled as he released the rope from the mooring, bundled and slipped it under the center seat then with the oars in hand, rowed clear of the surrounding boats.

"Absolutely. Raise the sail."

The wind rose and he tucked the oars away, gripped the ropes and with a grin, did as she'd bid. "Hold tight. The waves are choppy and it appears we're going to hit rough winds as we head around the tip into the open sea."

"Hold onto what?" she yelled over the sudden thrashing of the waves.

"The seat," Zenia called as she clasped hers.

The wind filled the sail with a hearty slap and the skiff shot off like an arrow. She squawked as the boat rose half out of the water on hers and James's side. She toppled into him.

"I've got you." He hauled her against his chest with one arm then planted his feet wide on the edge and leaned back farther to maintain the boat's balance. "Stay there, Zenia, where you're safe."

"This is wonderful." Zenia beamed.

"I've never sailed like this before." Arianna wrapped her

arms around his waist and clung as the wind sent their skiff flying across the water.

"The crosswinds can be tricky along this coast. They'll ease once we clear the point." He dropped a kiss on the top of her head. "Are you all right?"

"I am now." She relaxed and let go, knowing he'd hold her. If she wished, she could almost reach out and touch the white-capped waves with her hand.

"I'll keep a lookout for the stream," Zenia hollered as she eyed the shoreline.

"Aye, alert me to the spot where we are to make landfall." The wind whipped through James's shoulder-length auburn hair, giving it a rakish look she completely adored. As he held the ropes, his biceps bulged and his every muscle strained to control the wind power he'd harnessed in the skiff's tight sail. A warrior of great strength.

She stroked his broad shoulders and arms. "I wish I could sail with you more often." Plastered against the hard planes of his body, she smiled and lifted her face to the sky. "This is the way to live life, enjoying all Skye has to offer."

"You look so happy."

"I always am when I'm with you." She snuggled her cheek against his warm chest, although all too soon they rounded the tip and the wind eased. Waves splashed over the bow as the skiff settled down and James held the ropes and her as he jumped from the edge into the hull.

She scampered to her seat and patted her racing heart as she sat.

James tied the ropes off to hold the sail in place then dropped in beside her. With the rudder in hand, he guided them alongside the coastline. "Have you ever traveled to the north of Skye?"

"Yes, all the way to Trotternish at the tip. Dad and I lived to the south of Dunvegan, further along the inland channel of the loch. There are a number of Cunninghams with homes overlooking the sea, and our stone lodge was amongst them along the cliffs."

"He crafted weapons did he no'?"

"Yes, swords and shields, and chainmail and helms. He sold all he made for auction on the internet. His pieces fetched good money."

"What is the internet? I've no' heard you speak of that afore."

"It's hard to describe, but I'll try." Hmm, where did she even begin? "I want you to imagine a spider's web, all those intricate silken lines crossing at just the right point to create a net. Now take that net and widen it so it covers the entire world."

"So all the people on the Earth would be captured within it?"

"Exactly. The net is the internet or what is called the World Wide Web. Anyone can hook into it. You just need a device that can speak to all the other devices everyone holds. Information can be shared along the silken lines, or even through the air surrounding that web. With the entire world connected in such a way, Dad listed the pieces he created on this web and those interested in purchasing would place a bid."

"Anyone in the world could see what he wished to sell because of a spider's web?"

"Yes." She laughed and he chuckled.

"You have a vivid imagination, Arianna. One cannae see another without being near them."

"In the future one can even talk to someone else around the other side of the world on the tiniest of devices. You believe I traveled through time, yet you can't imagine the internet exists?"

"I believe all you say, but that still does no' mean I find it difficult to imagine." He cupped her cheek and stroked his thumb back and forth. "I enjoy hearing you speak of the future and your father. Your love for him is clear to see."

"I can't lose him." She turned her head into his touch and kissed his palm. "I can't wait to write him another letter and see it delivered to my home."

"Soon." He wrapped an arm around her shoulders and tucked her closer against his side. "You have my word I'll take you."

The wind whipped her hair in a frenzy and overhead, sent white wispy cloud streaming across the vivid blue sky. Along this expanse of rugged coastline, the forest drew right up to the water's edge.

"There's the stream," Zenia said from the bow. A trickling stream lay between the forest and a craggy hill topped with lush green grass. "I've never been to this exact spot. Have you, Arianna?"

"No. It's kind of off the beaten track in the future, unless one's sailing along these waters. Dad and I usually drove along the roads."

James adjusted the rudder and sent them cruising toward the edge of Rory's land. He lowered the sail and guided their boat into shore. As the skiff scraped the sand, he bounded out and roped the boat to a boulder. The waves rolled in and splashed his knees. "Come, Arianna. I'll carry you. Only one of us needs to get wet."

She nabbed her basket, climbed onto the seat then jumped into his arms.

He caught her with a chuckle. "You're clearly eager to be back on dry land."

"I love exploring new places."

"We have an hour, mayhap two afore we need to leave. The sword challenge event begins after the midday meal." He set her down on the beach then reached back for Zenia, caught her up and set her on her feet on the pebbly sand.

Zenia adjusted her basket over her arm and eyed Arianna. "I'll search the woods on the other side of the stream while you take this side. Collect what you can. Plenty of lavender if you find it, my dear." She glanced at James. "Stay with Arianna. I'll be fine on my own."

"I shall, provided you dinnae wander too far." James lent Zenia a steadying hand as he aided her across the shallow stream.

"Of course. I'll call out should I have need." She waved then disappeared into the trees.

"Are you ready?" He returned to her.

"Yes, we'll head to the top of the hill first." She wandered along the grassy trail winding upward, James keeping pace beside her. "I, ah, told Zenia about our connecting door this morning, and about your intention to court Margaret."

"I see."

"She said so many marriages these days are made in order to strengthen clan ties, that you're Donald MacDonald's nephew and your chief has never fathered any sons." She stopped at the top of the rise next to a wildflower patch, set her basket down and plucked what she needed. "I also told her we kissed."

"And what did she say?"

"That you aren't the kind of man to kiss just any lass."

"She's correct." He moved in behind her, providing solid warmth at her back. "What else did she say?"

"She understands that I can't bind myself to anyone here in this time, although she said I should still live my life. When Zenia lived here, she was betrothed to a warrior named Samuel Cunningham, a man she loved dearly. I learnt this morning they even spent one night together before he left for war, a war he never returned from." She pressed her palm against his chest. "I can't help but think that at least they'd had that one night together."

"What are you saying?"

"That I wouldn't mind having the same, one night with you before it's no longer possible." She'd experienced his kisses and she couldn't deny she wanted more, to steal a little happiness just for herself.

"One night with you would never be enough for me." He slid his arm around her waist, turned her and drew her against him, his chest to her back. Over her shoulder, he pointed ahead. "Look, Dunvegan is visible from here."

The castle guarded the mouth of Loch Dunvegan, and the waters before it shimmered a brilliant blue-green. Beyond, the Cuillin mountains rose majestically. "It's stunning, and you're trying to divert my attention."

"Aye, because I want you, Arianna." James swept her long hair to one side, dipped his head and nuzzled her nape.

"As I want you." She stretched against him and such peace settled in her soul. "I love being in your arms. It feels like home."

He nipped her skin then stepped back. "You are making it hard for me to walk away."

"I'm sorry, but we've always been honest with each other." She turned and cupped his cheek. "Will you think on my offer?"

"We're supposed to be collecting herbs."

"Well, that wasn't a direct no." Although she wouldn't press him anymore, but give him some time to consider her request. "We should continue on. Zenia will wonder what we've been doing if we return with nothing to show for all our time out here." She picked up her basket, looped it over her arm and continued along the trail collecting what she needed. Once done, she made her way back to the beach.

Zenia stood near the skiff sifting through her overflowing basket of herbs. She grinned as she glanced at them. "Oh, lovely. Your basket brims with goodies."

"I have plenty of lavender." Zenia used it for headaches, toothaches, sprains, sores, and so much more.

"Look what else I found in my search." Zenia held a cream fan-shaped shell for her to see, one with a pure white center in the shape of a heart. "It reminds me of one my mother and I once found. I'm going to keep this one."

"I love collecting shells. At the cove near my home, Dad and I used to collect shells for my mother then lay the prettiest one inside her memorial stone. That was our special place for her since we didn't have a grave."

"We'll collect one on the morrow if you like." James aided her aboard then Zenia. "On our way to your father's home."

"We're going tomorrow?"

"'Twill be the best time to do so. The foot races are being held then and that's an event I can easily miss." He boarded, nabbed the oars and sat on the center bench seat. He rowed until the breeze once again picked up then raised the sail, secured the ropes and dropped in beside her at the stern.

"Thank you. I can't wait." She smiled the entire way home as they make the return trip. Tomorrow couldn't come soon enough.

After James moored his skiff, he led them up the trail and into the keep. He dipped his head toward her. "I'll see you at the sword challenge event."

"You've got it, and be careful. No getting hurt." She lifted onto her toes and kissed his cheek. "Thank you for taking us out this morning. It was wonderful."

"You're welcome."

"Let's take these herbs to Mattie." Zenia walked into the side room off the great hall where the castle's healer worked and Arianna followed her. Zenia laid her herbs on the side table, tied some into bunches and hung them on a wire strung near the fireplace.

Arianna sorted through her haul and handed Zenia the bunches of plantain herb she'd collected. Zenia plucked the leaves from the stem and along with a stone mortar and pestle, mashed and ground the herb into a green paste, a concoction she used for cleansing wounds and preventing infection.

Arianna folded the clean cloths the maids had left and set them in a pile underneath the narrow window. Outside in the inner courtyard, the competing warriors, outfitted in their battle leathers, had gathered while many more watched from the sidelines. "The Games are about to begin."

"I've done all I need for now. We can go and watch." Zenia crossed to Mattie. "If you have need of us, call out."

"Aye, I shall." The elderly woman with a brown apron tied at her ample waist set a cauldron of water to boil on the fire and wiped her brow. "Enjoy yourselves."

"We will." Arianna hurried outside and edged through the chanting men. A tall burly warrior stomped to the center of the yard in thick fur boots and a gong in hand.

He swung his hammer against the metal and bellowed over the clanging. "Here ye. I hereby request the first two competitors to come forward. Round one will be clan MacDonald of Dunscaith against clan Cunningham of Glencairn. Your clan's strongest warrior shall fight."

James eyed William across the field of play.

William stepped forward and she held her breath as James did the same.

Oh no. This was not the pairing she wished to see.

Chapter 3

Fidgeting from foot to foot, Arianna wrung her hands together. The last two men she wished to see come up against each other were James and William, and certainly not in this event.

William strode toward the center of the inner courtyard, his tan padded cotun fastened over a white shirt and his belted plaid. His gaze clashed with James's, a fierce and fiery look that spoke of intended retribution.

From the sheath across his back, James slid his claymore free. He'd changed his vest and now wore a war coat over his black leather pants. He tipped his chin up and stared William down. "I look forward to our match. May the best warrior win."

"That shall be me." Teeth gritted, William withdrew his sword and circled James.

"Strong words, William." James softened his footing in preparation to attack. "You seem so certain."

"When you're ready, then begin," the overseer bellowed. "To the first who yields goes defeat."

William struck and James blocked. Their weapons clashed dead center, steel slamming hard against steel, the clang reverberating throughout the yard. "I'm always ready. What of you, MacDonald?"

"Aye, always. Ensure you dinnae hold back on my account."

William came at James, landing several solid blows one after the other, then twirled and attacked on James's other side, each hit stronger than the last.

"You show great strength." James was forced back with each strike.

"And I intend to show far more. You favor your right."

"I favor neither side." James switched sword hands and fought. He gained back the ground he'd lost, sweat gleaming on his brow as he met each of William's blows. "What of you?"

"I favor a win, however that may be achieved." William snorted. "Be prepared for defeat."

Battle lust rode them both hard, the itch to kill clear to see in the power behind each of their strikes. She teetered on her toes, hands clenched together. William swung his claymore down on James's blade, time and time again and James defended then struck himself. So evenly matched, in power, height, and skill.

All around the crowd cheered for one warrior or the other and she wanted to drown their booming demands out. So bloodthirsty.

James slammed his blade into William's side, slicing through his cotun.

Winded, William grunted. He grasped his side, though no blood seeped through.

"William." She rushed forward.

"Arianna, nay." Zenia clutched her hand and tugged her back. "You cannae distract either of them right now."

"They're going to kill each other. William will never allow a hit like that to go unpunished."

James shot a look at her. "Dinnae come any closer."

"Be careful." She hauled one arm free of Zenia. "Behind—"

William's sword blow knocked James onto his back then William swung again. James grappled to meet the attack, their blades crashing a mere inch from his nose. His arm shook as William's blade drew closer toward his neck. One breath would see cold steel slicing into his throat. "I returned from training to discover you and Arianna had enjoyed a wee sail this morn. I believe I made my wishes well and truly clear last eve. You're to leave her be."

"And I made my position clear as well." James's biceps bulged as he thrust and gained a second inch. "She is mine to protect." He kicked William's shin then rolled as William's blade crashed down and nearly nicked his ear.

"James, if you get one scratch on you, I'm going to be very angry." She'd had enough of this challenge.

"Aye, I'll take care, my imp." He shot to his feet, barely ducking William's next blow. "Cunningham, only the lowest of the low would use an innocent woman to gain ground in a fight."

"You are too easily distracted." He laughed.

"No' anymore." James slammed his blade home and William stumbled to one knee. Swiftly, he slid his claymore tight against William's throat. "Concede your defeat or I draw first blood."

"I concede naught."

"Then 'twill be done." He pressed until blood oozed and the overseer bellowed the match win in James's favor.

The MacDonald warriors rushed forward and lifted James high, their fists pumping into the air.

She raced to William's side but he shook his head, swiped the smear of blood clear and sheathed his sword. Hatred burned in his eyes as he glared at James. William intended his revenge and James would need to remain alert.

"Come. It may be better if we watch from inside." Zenia drew her away.

"I can't leave now. I need to warn James."

"James is well aware of William's intentions. The two have been fighting for years." She ushered her through the great hall and into the healer's side room.

"Good. You've both returned in time to aid me. Wonderful." Mattie lifted a lad of five or six onto the corner chair near the fireplace and on her knees before him, rolled his dusty brown breeches up and propped his leg on a short three-legged stool. Blood dripped from a nasty cut running down the boy's calf muscle.

"We'll wash our hands and be right with you." Zenia poured water into the basin and with a bar of soap, scrubbed her hands clean.

Arianna did the same then with another water basin, dipped a clean cloth and crouched next to the boy. She removed all sign of dirt, blood, and grime from around the wound.

"All will be well soon, Robert." Mattie inspected the cleaned wound. "It isnae too deep and Zenia made a special green paste earlier which will cleanse and heal you."

"It hurts." The lad with a mop of dark curls sniffed and tried to hold back his tears.

"No' for long." Zenia collected the pot of plantain paste she'd made and she and Mattie carefully smeared it along the length of the cut. "I believe this wound will heal by itself without any stitches. Binding it should be enough. What do you think, Mattie?" Zenia asked her.

"Aye, we'll bind it well." She arched a brow at Robert. "You must also take great care. Ye're no' allowed to get this wound wet."

"Aye, I'll be careful." A fat tear trickled down his dirt-smeared cheek.

"I'm sure you will." Zenia took a strip of clean cloth from the table and wrapped it firmly around the boy's leg then pinned the cloth in place. "Should you feel worse, even a smidgeon, I want you to return, no matter the hour."

"I will." His big green eyes widened. "The chief said you healed him when he was a lad and broke his arm and leg."

"I did, and he followed my instructions and all was well within no time at all. That's what I want you to do."

"I'll take you back to your mother, Robert." Mattie helped him to his feet then led him from the room.

Arianna tipped the dirty water out the window as the crowd applauded a MacIan warrior who'd won the next sword challenge against a MacDougall, his clansmen clapping his back with their congratulations. "Zenia, whenever James and William cross paths, war breaks out between them. There must be something I can do to bridge the gap and instill some peace."

"Those two men are both so strong-willed and fight for what they believe is right." She corked the pot of plantain paste and set it back on the table.

"Well said, Zenia." James strode into the room and planted himself in front of Arianna. He crossed his arms. "Never will you enter the field of play again. I'm well aware of when William attempts to distract me." He glanced over his shoulder at Zenia. "If you dinnae mind, I wish to speak to Arianna in private."

"Of course, but listen well to what she says. She holds only concern in her heart, for both you and William." She bustled out, bronze skirts in hand then shut the door behind her.

The antechamber's walls closed in, the space far smaller now James loomed over her.

His gaze narrowed. "My heart near burst from my chest when you attempted to enter the battle."

"My heart did when William tried to take your head off." She skimmed his forearms then dipped her fingers into the gap where they crossed. "He'd do so in a heartbeat if he could. I never want to witness such a fight between you both again."

"Men fight. 'Tis the way of the world."

"Not the way you two just did. William hates you, and now

more so than ever before."

"He may hate me, but he'll also be less arrogant the next time we cross paths."

"How can you be so sure?"

"Because if our positions had been reversed, I would have learnt my lesson well from the match that just played out. A worthy warrior never underestimates his opponent." He stroked a finger under her chin as he looked deep into her eyes. "As I shall learn not to underestimate you."

* * * *

James stepped Arianna back until she came up against the wall then pressed his hands on the cool stone either side of her head. "After that match, one thing has now become abundantly clear."

"And that is…"

"Even in the midst of a battle, you wouldnae hesitate to come to my defense, just as I would never hesitate to come to yours. You asked for one night afore it's no longer possible, and this is my answer. I wish to court you."

"What?"

"I realize your desire is to return to your father and not be held to this time by any other." He touched his nose to hers. "I've been a fool to think I can set you aside and court another woman. I'd rather have whatever time we're granted together than none at all."

"You have a dream, to unite the clans and bring about some peace. I'm not closely enough aligned to Rory for that to happen."

"Your close ties to the Cunninghams will aid me in bringing about a little of that peace I seek. Regardless, I cannae keep denying what lies between us."

"You need a wife who'll consider your interests first, not those of another. I'd return to my father in a heartbeat if I could."

"If that so happened, then your leaving would be for the

right reason, one I couldnae dispute." He lowered his head to the curve of her neck and brushed his lips over her skin. "Arianna, I will never be complete without you."

"I'll never be complete without you either, but—"

"I'm glad you agree." He settled his mouth over her pulse and sucked, hard.

Her knees wobbled. "You're not fighting fair."

He released her skin, nibbled across her neck to the other side and sucked again. "Say aye and give me your agreement to a courtship. I want everyone to know you're mine, including William."

She sank her hands into his hair and sighing, arched her body into his. "I need some time to think about this."

"Then you have until tonight." He wouldn't wait any longer. He trailed his lips lower, down her neck and along the low-cut neckline of her gown. Her nipples beaded and poked the silvery-blue satin. He cupped her breasts and thumbed the peaks through the fabric. She was so responsive. "May I touch you?"

"You already are." She latched onto his shoulders.

"Nay, I've barely begun to touch you. I need to kiss you and it cannae wait any longer." He covered her mouth with his and kissed her, until the taste of her swarmed his senses. He slipped the edge of her bodice to one side, eased his hand inside and filled his palm with her warm flesh.

"Oh, that feels wonderful. Don't stop."

Heat surged into his loins and he kissed her deeper. He plunged his tongue inside her mouth and drank in her sweet nectar. 'Twas a losing battle to keep his passion in check now she'd unleashed his desire for her, and even more so when she entwined her tongue with his and drove him beyond his endurance in a delicious dance.

More. He wanted more, and not just to have his hand against her. He dipped his head and grazed his teeth over her nipple. Her lush, warm breast taunted him to take more. He rolled his tongue around the peak and drew her nipple deep inside his mouth.

"James." She moaned, her fingers biting into his shoulders. "I love how you touch me."

"I love it more." He gave her other breast equal attention. He lapped the tight bud, gorging himself on the woman he'd adored for so long.

"Arianna, James." A knock sounded on the door.

Zenia's voice penetrated the fog in his head. He pulled back and fought for a breath.

"I'm sure I said don't stop." Arianna clutched his cheeks, her eyes hazed with passion. "I want more."

"Zenia's at the door."

"What?" She gasped and yanked her gown up. "I—I didn't hear her."

"I'll go. There are four further rounds afore the final sword challenge, events I dinnae wish to miss. We'll talk this eve, in your chamber." He dropped a quick kiss on her lips. "I intend to sway you to my way of thinking then."

A fire now raged within him, one Arianna had stirred to blazing life. Aye, he'd accept no other. Not now. Not ever.

* * * *

As the sun hovered on the horizon, Arianna stood amidst the crowd. James had won each of his subsequent four rounds and now took his position as one of the two warriors competing in the final. The other man was the reigning champion, Rory MacLeod, and he stood in wait, his claymore snug in his hand as he twirled it in a wide figure eight.

Across the courtyard, James hauled his damp war coat off and donned a fresh steel-studded black cotun.

Arianna dragged in a deep breath and tried to still her racing heartbeat.

"Are you all right?" Zenia rubbed her arm.

"It's just as well I've never had to watch him head into

battle before now. I can barely stand to see him fighting like this and these are only the Games."

"He's represented his clan well. Whether he wins this final round or no', he's gained the respect of many of the warriors here."

James turned his gaze on her and the look of scorching need in his eyes burned into her. He'd now stamped his claim on her and she desperately wanted to bend to his will, to say yes to a courtship and anything he asked. Touching him, being with him, it was what she wanted no matter how much time remained for her in the past.

"Take your places," the overseer boomed as the last lantern was lit on the curtain wall to ward off the impending dark. "The final sword challenge begins."

The crowd cheered.

Goodness. She was never going to survive this final round.

* * * *

The overseer's gong rang and James thrust his sword high and blocked MacLeod's fierce blow. "I see you dinnae intend to waste a moment of this challenge, Rory."

"'Tis been too long since I last battled a MacDonald." Rory came at him, slashing again and again in a clear attempt to take him down as quick as he could. "The hour also grows late and my belly rumbles for the celebratory feast that awaits."

"I dinnae intend to make this match an easy one." He sprang forward and fought. 'Twas time for clan MacDonald to take the sought after sword championship title this year and with Arianna watching, he had no greater incentive than to fight for her, to ensure she knew he would be able to protect her no matter who his adversary was. He wanted a future with her, and only her, and he damn well wished he'd seen that far sooner.

From the sidelines, MacLeod warriors cheered their chief on and Rory's gaze glinted with determination as he slammed his blade into James's, one hard strike after the other.

James grunted and fell back a step. "It looks like I'll need to be quicker on my feet around you."

"You're welcome to try." Rory twirled his blade and circled him, then advanced and forced James back even further. His strategic blows, with one coming to one side and then the other, were worked in an attempt to weaken him.

Enough. He needed to attack rather than defend. He rocked on his heels, blocked Rory's next fierce blow, then dropped low and rolled clear of his adversary and the circle of Rory's warriors pressing heavily in on his back. Now with his own men behind him, their cheers ringing loud in his ears, he met Rory's next strike with the same intensity as the reigning champion heaved on him.

"James!" Arianna shouted as she ran across the clearing, her golden tresses streaming behind her. "Not a scratch. Do you hear me?"

"Stay back." He glared at Artair. "Keep her beside you."

Rory struck his ribs and pain ricocheted and rattled his teeth from the brutal blow. Arianna screamed as Rory swung again.

He barely caught the next strike and arms shaking, shoved his two-handed sword hard against Rory's and sprang forward and fought. As Rory pulled his sword back, James slammed his blade into Rory's arm and sliced through his padded coat.

Rory gritted his teeth as blood seeped through and stained the thick rawhide. "Damn it," he spat.

"James MacDonald has drawn first blood," the overseer bellowed and swung his hammer into the gong. A piercing clang ricocheted through the courtyard.

James's men bounded from the crowd and lifted him high into the air.

Arianna ran to him and he jumped from his high perch and caught her in his arms. "You did it." She clasped his face and beamed. "My champion."

"Aye," he rasped, his heartbeat a raging mess. "I cannae

believe it. 'Twas a lucky strike."

The crowd surged and he was pulled away and swept back onto his warriors' shoulders.

Euphoria overflowed him and he punched his fist into the air as Rory dipped his head in acknowledgement toward him. James nodded and called out to one and all. "My thanks to Rory MacLeod for a hard and fast fight. May we never meet on the battlefield, but only over ale and fine food."

"To ale and fine food!" Rory raised his sword. Even in defeat, the MacLeod chief showed great honor. "Let's celebrate MacDonald's win with the feast that awaits."

Chapter 4

Warriors surged into the great hall from the inner courtyard and Arianna moved with the flow.

At the dais, Rory called all to order and as the hall went quiet, he beckoned James forward, clapped him on the back and said, "A worthy win to James MacDonald. He caught me quite unaware."

Applause reverberated and Margaret leaned closer to Arianna, her gown's forest-green skirts brushing hers. "Rory was concerned about only one other competitor going into the sword challenge event and that was James." Margaret nodded. "Now I see why. James never gave up the fight, even when it appeared Rory had the advantage."

She squeezed Margaret's hands. "Your brother is an honorable chief and warrior."

"Aye, and I thank you for saying so." Clear admiration bloomed on her face. "I must tell him how well he fought. Excuse me." She hurried toward Rory and hugged him.

So many emotions rolled through Arianna, elation for James's win and worry that it all could have gone so differently. Overwhelmed, she swayed and grasped the chair before her.

"Arianna, are you all right?" Zenia caught her arm and

pressed the back of her hand against her forehead and cheeks. "You're rather clammy."

"I just need a moment to breathe."

"Come, I'll take you to your chamber." Zenia steered her upstairs and into her room. She pulled out the seat from in front of the desk and sat her in it. "I'll prepare an herbed drink and bring you a tray. You have no' eaten since this morn. It'll help to restore you."

"Yes, please. I'd like that."

"Is all well?" James strode in. "I saw you leave with Arianna."

"She simply needs some nourishment and a moment to rest." Zenia bustled toward him and smiled. "My congratulations. You fought so very well."

"Thank you."

"Look after Arianna for me." She squeezed his shoulder. "I willnae be long."

"Of course." He closed the door after she left and crossed to her, his gaze worried. "What's wrong, imp?"

"I'm so sorry. I lost my wind for a moment. You don't have to stay, not with the festivities underway. Go and celebrate your win."

"If you have need of me then I'll remain right here." A cold wind blew through the window and James closed it. "Let me rid this chamber of its chill." He removed his cotun and tossed it onto the corner gold and silver striped padded chair. He knelt at the hearth, his white shirt stretched taut over his broad shoulders as he bent to the task. Quickly and precisely, he pulled stringy bark off a log, struck flint with his dirk, and coaxed the sparks to life then built the fire into a crackling blaze with twigs and wood from the basket. Over his shoulder, he glanced at her. "You're looking less pale already."

"The room is warming up nicely, and having you here without a sword in your hand and watching someone trying to slice you into bits helps.”

“I see.” He grinned.

“You like to fight too much.” She tut-tuttered under her breath.

“And you like to argue too much.”

A rap sounded and Zenia bustled in and placed a tray of hot food and a steaming cup of her promised herbal tea on the desk before her. “I’m afraid I cannae stay. Mattie needs aid tending one of the warriors who suffered an injury in the sword challenges. His wound is deeper than he first believed.”

“Go. I’ll remain with Arianna.” James poured water from the jug into the basin.

“Thank you, James. There’s plenty enough food on this tray for both of you.” Zenia kissed her cheek. “If you have need of me, send a maid with a message and I’ll return immediately.”

“Thank you.”

“Now eat.” She pointed at the tray.

“Yes, Mother.”

“Cheeky lass.” Zenia tweaked her nose then left.

James closed the door and bolted it behind her. He loosened his tunic’s laces, drew his shirt over his head and dipped a cloth in the basin of water and wiped his arms and chest. His golden skin gleamed in the firelight.

“I’m not sure it’s a good idea for you to wander about my chamber shirtless.”

“You’re supposed to be eating.”

“I can’t eat when you’re parading around half naked.” She picked up her fork, stabbed a slice of beef and waved it at him. “All those muscles of yours are completely distracting.”

“I need to stay.” He leaned closer, hands either side of the arms of her chair as he bit the meat from the end of her fork and chewed. “’Tis delicious. You should try some.”

“That was my piece.”

“Then allow me to feed you.” He snuck her fork from her

hand, chose a piece of salmon from the tray and slipped the morsel between her lips.

The delectable flavor of the fresh fish melted in her mouth.

"Do you remember that time I first took you fishing?" He fed her another piece.

"I'll never forget. You taught me how to bait a hook, toss a line and make a grand catch, and all while I had only the use of one arm." They'd spent so much time together at the stream near Zenia's cottage. He'd had to carry her about until her broken bones had mended.

"Aye, you hopped up and down on one foot and squealed with delight when you made your first catch. Your excitement brought back such sweet memories from the time I'd first fished with my father. There is naught more exciting than catching one's first fish."

After she'd hauled her catch in, he'd skinned and boned it, then threaded it onto a sturdy stick and cooked it over an open fire." They'd sat there for hours, talking until the moon had risen and the hour grown late.

"What are you thinking?" He stabbed a cube of roasted carrot with the fork and popped it in her mouth before eating some himself.

"You surprised me that day. You were so relaxed and content to do nothing more than entertain a young girl when you had far more important things to do. You delayed seeing to your chief's request because of me."

"'Twas important I stayed and glad I am that I did. You needed the aid. Which reminds me." He set the fork down, foraged in the drawer then pulled out a piece of paper, a quill, and ink. "You should write your father's letter now. I'd like to leave first thing in the morn for your home."

"Thank you." She dipped the quill into the ink then wrote her letter. She penned precise instructions so Dad would know exactly what illness was coming. He'd been only a few months too late in getting his cancer diagnosed. He needed to seek medical treatment with plenty of time to spare. He had to live. For her.

As she'd done with all the letters she'd written him in the past, she told him of her trip through time and gave him as much information as she could about all that had happened since she'd arrived. So too she wrote about some of the precious things they'd done together over the years, those special occasions they'd marked so when he read her letter, he'd know it'd come from her. Lastly, she asked him not speak to her about her trip through time for fear it'd change her first jump and her ability to aid him. Once done, she signed her name and blew on the ink until it dried, folded it in three and sealed it with red wax and the MacLeod stamp from the drawer.

"All done?" James sat next to her after adding another log to the fire and nudged her herbed tea toward her.

"Yes. I've covered everything, just as I've done with my past letters. Surely one of them will reach him." She sipped her drink. "Can you keep this safe for me until we arrive at the lodge?"

"Of course." He pocketed the letter, his blue gaze so hungry and needy as he seized the sides of her chair and scraped her around so she faced him again. "Now we need to talk."

"Put on a shirt and we will."

"I think no'." He caught her around the waist and set her astride him on his lap, her silvery-blue skirts bunched between them. Looking deep into her eyes, he murmured, "You asked for a night with me and I intend to give you one filled with pleasure, and following that, a lifetime of nights all exactly the same. First though, I need to hear your agreement." He stroked along her outer thighs and as he did, he slid her hem higher and exposed her legs. "Say aye to a courtship."

"I can't think straight when you touch me like that."

"That would be my preference." He kissed her, his lips

moving over hers with heat and thorough attention. "'Tis past time for us to deepen our bond, for me to show you exactly what you mean to me."

"You make it impossible for a girl to say no." She spread her palms over his wide chest. His deliciously smooth skin held a smattering of hair, the same glorious shade as his auburn head. His muscles rippled as she touched him, so strong and unyielding. All warrior. All man. All hers.

"More than fate brought us together that day you first arrived through time. I wasnae only traveling to Edinburgh, but also to you." He dipped a finger down her neck and along her gown's square-cut neckline. "I need to undress you."

"Yes, please." She couldn't halt her need, or what would come to pass between this night.

"Perfect." He rose to his feet and set her on hers, then hands on her shoulders, gently turned her around and unlaced her gown. He smoothed the satin down over her sark until it fell in a swish to her ankles, then scooping her into his arms, he carried her to the bed and laid her on the soft brown fur covering.

"Can I undress you too?"

"After I'm done with you." He gripped the hem of her ankle-length undergarment and slowly slid the white linen up her legs. The fabric skimmed her outer thighs, her hips, and torso. "Lift your arms."

She did and he drew the fabric over her head and tossed it to the end of the bed.

"You're so beautiful." His hot gaze raked her body then he leaned over her and with one finger, traced around her beading nipples. "I need to taste you."

"I'm all yours."

"Aye, all mine." He eased her breasts together and dipped his head. The raspy stroke of his tongue across the sensitive tips sent a bolt of pleasure to her core.

"You're over dressed, James." She fumbled with the ties of

his pants. "Take these off."

He kicked his boots free and grabbed his loosened waistband. Swiftly, he shoved the leather down his thickly muscled legs and off.

Her mouth watered as his cock bobbed free and brushed his belly, one very large cock with a plump head. Gently, she tip-toed her fingers down his chest and along the thin trail of hair that thickened into a darker thatch of curls covering the apex of his groin. "I might never have made love to a man before, but I'm a twenty-first century woman and I know what I want."

"And what is that, my imp." He knelt between her legs and his balls drew tighter and higher, his shaft thickening and lengthening further.

"You. Deep inside me, and the two of us joined in the most beautiful of ways."

"Aye, that is what I want too." He feasted his gaze on her below. "I intend to bind you to me for all time."

"You already have." A myriad of emotions tumbled through her. Desire, longing, and a throbbing need. She wanted to experience it all, and only with him. "I want you, except I've no idea how to make everything work when my dream is to return home."

"Dinnae think of home, only this moment. Touch me."

She ran her thumb across his warm lips. His body was all finely honed muscle and heat, and she adored him, but his soft mouth drew her. Dizzy, and a little breathless, she murmured, "That first day after I awoke in Zenia's cottage, I was so frightened by all that had happened, but with you there holding and reassuring me, that terror faded away. Being with you, knowing you were close, calmed me in a way I've only ever felt with you."

"I will always be close. No further separation, from this day forth." He bent his head, his hands sweeping under her bottom as he pressed a soft kiss to her belly. "I want you to relax and give yourself over to me."

She stretched her arms over her pillowed head, her trust in him absolute.

"Good." He raised her legs, hooked them over his shoulders until her bottom lifted off the bed and she lay fully exposed to him. "You're so pink and lush, a meal of indescribable beauty."

"What are you going to do?"

"'Tis best I show you, because I intend to take what is mine, heart, body, and soul." Grinning, he caressed along her inner thighs, parted her folds and plunged one finger deep inside her. Pleasure ricocheted outward from her core and hardened her already hard nipples further. "I see you like that." His grin widened.

"I love it, and I imagine there's nothing you'll do that I won't absolutely adore."

He stroked inside her harder and faster, then rubbed his thumb across her nub until she arched into his touch. "Are you ready for more?"

"Yes," she panted. "Anything and everything."

"I intend to make you scream my name." He added a second finger then dipped his head. He licked her flesh then kissed her in the most intimate way as he thrust both fingers in. Such exquisite pleasure radiated through her core and rippled outward, tingling her fingers and toes. In a deep and delicious rhythm, he moved, every flick of his tongue and stroke of his fingers making her gasp and strive for a peak that lay so temptingly close. Her desire built, higher and higher.

"James." Before she lost her mind, she searched and skimmed the hard length of his cock. Instinct took over and she caressed his hot flesh, pumping him in time with how he stroked her.

He moaned, long and low. "Cease. Too much."

"I need more, to have your mouth on mine, to be covered by you." Every glorious inch of him. "Please, kiss me."

He lifted up, took her mouth in a hot kiss even as he continued to rub his fingers into her so completely and perfectly below.

"That feels exquisite." She stroked him harder, until an orgasm beckoned and she teetered on the verge of a precipice she could barely hold onto. Her hips moved of their own accord, rising again and again to meet his thrusting fingers. "I need you, James."

"Aye, 'tis time." Hands on her hips, he slowly, carefully, moved between her legs and nudged his cock along her slick folds. A deliciously decadent smile lifted his lips, his gaze hot and hungry. "Open wider for me. I want to be inside you, now."

She spread her legs farther. "Whatever you do, don't stop."

"It will hurt, just a little, and I cannae take that pain away." He teased his cock over her nub. "Although I'll do everything I can to make this good, to have you pining for more as soon as I can."

"I trust you." She cupped his face, looked into his eyes. "I always have and I always will."

"'Tis a trust I hold dear." He kissed her, sucking at her lower lip until liquid heat surged through her core. Then he deepened their kiss and demanded a response which distracted her mind. Swiftly, he pushed against the barrier, tore through and immersed himself deep inside her.

She gasped, her cry muffled against his neck as she held on fiercely tight, her legs quivering as she wrapped them around him. "I feel so full."

"'Tis done. Look at where we're joined." He lifted up just enough for her to see. "We're one and shall never be parted again."

"That's so beautiful." She clutched his butt as tortuously sweet sensations thrummed through her. "Make me fly. Give me everything you promised."

"I wish to give you all of me." With one hand on her hip, he eased back then so slowly pushed all the way back in. She moaned, and he increased his pace until her thoughts were consumed by him, the sensation of his body sliding deep into hers, all she desired. He pounded, harder and faster and she met each of his thrusts with one of her own.

"So good." She raked her fingers down his back, seized his warm skin then screamed his name just as he'd promised her she would. Adrift with pleasure, her inner muscles tightened and dragged him in.

"You're my woman," he moaned as he shuddered and spilled his seed deep, his release as strong and as all-consuming as hers. He rocked on top of her. "One I intend to keep for all time, safe in my heart and safe in my arms."

"Yes," she murmured. "For all time."

* * * *

James worked to calm his heaving heartbeat. An innumerable number of sensations had stormed through him as he'd pushed through Arianna's maidenhead and claimed her for himself. Then her body had dragged him in and pulsed around him, taking not only his very essence but also his heart.

"That felt incredible." She caught his face between her hands and pulled his mouth back to hers. Her kiss, so sweetly seductive, stirred his shaft back to life. "And so thrilling, like nothing I could've ever imagined joining as one would be."

"Now your body has accepted mine, 'twill be far easier for you the next time." He kissed her and she kissed him back with a primal heat that said she still wanted more. She was so alluring with her beautiful creamy skin and luscious pouty lips. "I must withdraw. I dinnae wish to hurt you."

"No." She wrapped her arms around his neck and held him in place. "In case you missed it, I love the feel of you inside me."

"Aye, as I adore it too, but there will be blood. I tore your maidenhead. Allow me to take care of you." He eased from her, rinsed out a cloth in the basin of water and gently removed all sign of their joining.

"You're smiling."

He touched his lips and grinner wider. "Aye, you've gifted me with what belongs to your husband, and that shall be me."

"Is that right?" she quizzed and nabbed his hand. She tugged him onto the mattress, pushed him onto his back and crawled on top of him. Every inch of her glorious body was on stunning display as she sat across his hips and wriggled against his groin, rubbing her slit over the base of his cock wedged between them. Her breasts swayed, heavy and full and demanding his attention. "Do you see something you like?"

"Aye, though you'll be too sore for more." Slowly, he grazed a finger from between her breasts to her belly, and as her breathing quickened, he trailed lower, swirled through the golden blond curls covering her entrance and rubbed her nub.

"That feels incredible and not one bit sore." Back arched, she covered his hand with hers and held him in place. "You have a magical touch."

"You truly wish for more?"

"I do, as well as much more of you. I want to taste you as you tasted me." On her belly, she squirmed down between his legs and slid her hand around his cock. With her breasts settling softly either side of his balls, her nipples grazing his flesh, she lifted one curious eyebrow as she eyed his shaft. "I believe I shall enjoy this."

"Are you certain you wish to take me in your mouth?"

"Very certain. Let me know if I do something you don't like." Peeking through her long lashes, she licked him in one long teasing stroke from root to tip then swirled her tongue around the head.

He groaned. "I like."

"Then I'm doing this right?" She cupped his balls and caressed them, then with a grin, settled her lips over his head and took him deep.

"Very right." He lifted his hips, his cock hardening impossibly further as her sweet mouth seared him. Such seductive torture, of the kind he wished to endure for a lifetime. He stretched under her touch, his shaft lengthening as a shimmer of heat blazed at his spine. "Arianna, you need to stop. I dinnae wish to come in your beautiful mouth."

"You taste delicious, and I'm enjoying this far too much to stop." She sucked him harder and he pushed deeper inside her mouth.

A sexual haze consumed him and he cradled her head in his hands and rocked his hips, demanding she take more of him. She did, then lifted up and rimmed the very tip of him with her mouth, giving him just enough of a reprieve to gain some much needed control. Aye, he would see to her pleasure again and ensure she experienced all he could offer her before he allowed himself to come. He flipped her over and caught her giggle with his lips. Kissing her, he explored the delicious recesses of her mouth then scooting down, planted his head between her creamy thighs and plundered the decadent bounty that awaited him there. "Open wider for me."

She gasped but widened her legs. "I feel too much already."

"Turnabout is fair play." Her inner flesh, lit by the glow of the flickering flames, sent a golden wash over the pink and he played his tongue over the tiny nub plumping delectably. "Brace yourself, my love. I intend to enjoy the spoils of my victory and get my fill of you this night."

Blood pounding, he took her clit between his lips and sucked. He lavished attention on her until she grasped the bedcover and moaned. She lifted her hips, seeking more and he reached up and tweaked her nipples, the tips so incredibly hard and pointy. He needed a taste of those too. He rose overtop and adored every lush inch of her breasts, ensuring her pleasure was absolute.

"James, too much, too much," she gasped, her back arching

as she pressed those luscious morsels even deeper into his mouth.

"Give yourself over to me, Arianna." He teased his teeth over each sensitive tip then swirled with his tongue until fire raced through his blood.

"I can't hold on any longer. Please, come inside me."

"Are you certain you're no' too sore?" His cock hammered at him to take her again. Everything within him demanded the joining, the feel of her heat wrapped around him and those tiny muscles of hers squeezing his flesh in the most beautiful of ways. He wanted to come, to experience the pleasure of her body rising to meet his and wring him dry.

"Inside me. Now." She clutched his butt and dragged him to her entrance.

His shaft grazed the folds of her hot flesh and he couldn't hold back. He thrust within and dove deep. She was his and there could be no denying either of them.

He pounded and she bucked.

His balls tightened, his cock twitching. She was so wet and he needed to satisfy her, to make her soar and to have her sweep him right along with her.

"James." She cried out his name as she thrashed underneath him, then she came, her inner muscles clamping down and dragging his cock in even deeper, right where he belonged in the heart of her.

"You're mine, always mine," he growled as he came in a hot rush he hadn't a chance of halting.

"Yes, as you're mine." Her body pulsed around him, drowning him in her heat, each erotic pull a claim on his soul. Never would he allow her to leave his side again.

"Mmm," she murmured as her eyelids drifted down.

"Sleep if you wish."

"I'm…" She yawned. "I'm…"

Sleep took her and slowly he pulled out then tucked her

safely against him.

"I need you, Arianna. More than my next breath," he whispered in her ear, a vow he'd prove to her was true.

So content with her in his arms, he gave in and allowed sleep to claim him too.

Chapter 5

Early morning sunshine streamed through the wooden shutters over Arianna's narrow window and woke her far sooner than she wished. She wriggled, her lower body trapped by James's muscled leg where he lay half over top of her, his arm curled around her waist. She smiled. He slept so soundly that not even her movement had awoken him.

A beam of sunlight trickled over the glistening ends of his fiery shoulder-length locks and across his high cheeks. His broad shoulders, so wide and thick with muscle, enticed her and she couldn't help but touch. She caressed his golden skin and smoothed down over his rigid biceps. All hers. She kissed his shoulder then nibbled along his neck and nipped his bottom lip. His breathing stopped, held as if he awaited her next move. The words embedded deep in her heart, slipped free. "I love you, James."

His long black lashes lifted and his eyes, the blue so smolderingly hot, melted her inside. "Say that again," he demanded.

"I love you." She planted her hands on his shoulders, pushed him onto his back then rolled on top of him. She crossed her arms over his chest, pressed her breasts against the light smattering of his chest hair, her blond locks falling in a silken curtain either side of his body. "And only you."

"I have more love for you in my heart than I can ever contain within it." He sank one hand into her hair, palmed the back of her head and drew her mouth to his. He kissed her, a slow and leisurely exploration that made her feel every inch of that love. "I desire none other than you, Arianna. I wish to care and provide for you throughout all of our days."

"I wish I could wake up next to you every single morning." She laid a finger over his mouth. "We need to talk, to come to an agreement."

"I would never ask you to choose between your father and me." He rolled to his side and settled her on her back. Gently, he skimmed his hand down her body and stroked her belly. "But neither will I ever suffer a separation from you."

"I don't wish to suffer a separation from you either." She cupped his face, lifted up the scant inch separating them and kissed him. He was the man she longed to spend the rest of her life with, only how could she have it all?

"Arianna?" A knock sounded. William.

She let out a loud sigh. "I swear he has the worst timing."

"I'll leave so you may speak to him." He swung his legs out of the bed, drew his pants and shirt on then swiped his cotun from overtop of the chair. He planted one fast kiss on her lips. "I shall see you down on the landing. I'll ready the skiff and ensure I have all the provisions we need. We sail for your father's home the moment you're ready."

"Thank you."

James whisked behind the ambry's golden curtain and disappeared.

She couldn't wait to see the lodge in its original form, and to talk to one of her father's direct ancestors. Not that James would allow her to speak of her circumstances, but she'd do whatever she could to ensure her letter reached her father. There must be someplace there she could safely stow it where her father would find it. He'd restored parts of the lodge when she'd been a child and he knew every inch of it, but she needed to find a place that meant something special just to them. Perhaps her mother's memorial stone. It sat right on the edge of the bluff in front of their home. The sacred stone held a cavity within, one well protected from the elements with a strong casing overtop. It was where they placed her mother's shells.

"Arianna, are you there?" Another knock.

"Just a minute, William."

She bounded out of bed, rummaged in her trunk for a nightrail and tugged it on. After snatching the fur cover from the bed, she wrapped it around her then opened the door. "Good morning."

William leaned against the doorway in tan pants and a black tunic, his Cunningham plaid draped over one shoulder. "'Tis unlike you to rise so late. Father and our warriors have already broken their fast and prepare to leave. I'm on my way to the sea-gate. We sail for the field of play just beyond the village. We can wait if you wish to travel with us."

"Has Rory MacLeod left?"

"Nay, no' yet."

"Then you go right on ahead and Zenia and I can catch a ride with him." She kissed his cheek. "I wouldn't want you to miss the foot races because I slept in."

"Aye, this is one event I shall win. I'll see you at the field." He slid one thumb through his belt hook and sauntered down the hallway.

"Load the birlinn with enough provisions for all. We've competing warriors and guests to feed." Rory's booming voice filtered through the closed window, ringing with authority from the lower courtyard.

She closed the door, tossed her fur cover onto the bed then hopped across the cold polished planks and crawled onto the wooden trunk's engraved lid. She flipped her nightrail's hem over her dangling feet to keep them warm then opened the shutters.

Outside, the morning sun's golden rays bathed the treetops and the green hills rising in the distance. The isles were stunning with their glistening lochs and bens and moors. Along the water's edge, the ocean's waves crashed into shore and seagulls squawked and took flight. Near the curtain wall, two maids in pale blue kirtles knelt at the edge of the green garden and pulled weeds. Children played nearby, chasing each other across the grass and around the ivy covered well. Barefoot and flush faced, their giggles floated toward her.

In her younger years, she'd run around those very gardens too, skipping and laughing. Dad had watched on, his smile wide. He'd always said her mother's MacLeod blood in her was strong, that here she belonged.

"We're almost done, lads. Bring the loaves of bread from the cook's kitchen and store them in the birlinn where they willnae get wet." Dressed in a loose white tunic and boots, his great plaid secured around his hips and pinned at his chest, Rory strode toward the arched stone tunnel leading down to the sea-gate entrance.

Two lanky lads dashed out from the side entrance, bread loaves stuffed within their arms. Both boys had red hair and breeches three or four inches too short on their legs. Knocking elbows and ribbing each other, they chased Rory into the tunnel.

From the front entrance, James stepped outside and she held her breath. Black leather pants hugged his trim hips and curved over his gloriously tight butt. His equally dark shirt fluttered free and as the breeze stirred, it lifted his hem and gave glimpses of golden skin she itched to touch again. One night wouldn't be long enough for her either, a fact, deep in her heart, she'd always known.

"Arianna, 'tis me." Zenia knocked then walked in with a

swish of her olive skirts, her lacy white shawl draped over her shoulders. Wide-eyed, she stopped. "Oh my, James just assured me you were up and he would be taking us to your father's home. Why are you no' dressed?"

"I'm reminiscing." She scampered off the trunk. "I have news. James has given up his quest of courting Margaret. We even came to an agreement of sorts last night."

"That sounds rather interesting." A smile lifted her lips as she crossed to her ambry and pulled out a deep blue riding habit and broad-brimmed hat. "Do tell."

"We've agreed we won't suffer a separation from each other."

"Are you speaking of marriage?"

"That's what James would like, and what I would too, although I've no idea how to make it all work with my desire to return to the future. He insists that doesn't matter and he'll accept whatever time we have together as it is." She tugged her nightrail over her head then folded it under her pillow.

"Life isnae always meant to be easy, but one should always follow their heart."

"My heart longs for everything, my father and James." She donned the white shirt Zenia handed her then tugged on the fitted jacket. The riding habit's skirt was long and full, cumbersome and weighty, but the extra layers would keep her warm outside on the water. She laced her leather boots as a rap sounded.

Zenia walked to the door and opened it.

"I have the tray you asked for." A serving maid dipped her head.

"Wonderful." Zenia motioned for her to enter. "On the side table, please."

The maid placed the tray where asked and took the one from last night with her as she left.

"I ordered porridge and oatcakes for us both." Zenia pulled out a chair and sat.

"Just what I need. I'm famished." She dropped into the chair opposite Zenia and poured their tea. Spoon in hand, she ate the porridge and it quickly warmed her belly.

Zenia munched on an oatcake, her blue eyes shining bright. "I imagine James will woo you with dedicated fierceness now you've come to your 'agreement.'" She smiled and sighed. "I remember those days of courtship. I miss my Samuel and—" Her smile suddenly died away.

"What's wrong?" She squeezed Zenia's hand. "You miss your Samuel and…"

"So much time has passed and I rarely speak of—" She shook her head as tears pooled in her eyes. "There is something I've never told you. The one night Samuel and I had together, we conceived a child, a bairn I gave birth to after his passing."

"Why didn't you say? I would have listened and understood."

"I know you would have, but my babe never even had the chance to take her first breath." More tears flowed and she wiped her cheeks. "She was such a wee lass with a mop of blond hair like her father's. The day I felt the pains coming over me, I felt driven to be closer to him even though that was impossible. So instead I boarded one of the skiffs sailing from here to Dunvegan Village then hired a horse when I reached the settlement and rode to the place where Samuel and I had spent so many wonderful times together. When the pains tightened my belly and I could no longer walk, I laid down and pushed." More tears fell. "When she came into this world, no' one noise did she even make."

"She was stillborn?" Her own tears fell and she left her chair and knelt before Zenia and grasped her hands. "I'm so sorry. You should never have had to go through that alone."

"The cord was wrapped tight around h-her n-neck." Her shoulders shook as she sobbed. "She was so cold and I couldnae bear the loss. I opened a portal and made a wish that she'd find her way safely to her father's arms, that he would care for her as I no longer could. Her body wavered afore my eyes and then she vanished. A lost soul, freed."

"You didn't even have a body to bury?"

"Nay, and I grieved for her for so long. With all I'd lost that year, my mother, Samuel and then my babe, I could no longer stay. I left Skye and the ghosts of my past behind. I'd hoped to find a fresh start and mayhap the love of my paternal clan." She cupped Arianna's cheek as a weak smile lifted her lips. "I found that, and then I found you."

"I'm so glad I traveled to you." Another tear slipped down her cheek. "You've always told me that the souls you free travel to where their light shines brightest. You are my light and so is James. You were both there that day I arrived for a reason."

"Aye, we were there for you." Her gaze softened. "That is why I now implore you to seek with James what your heart desires. One never knows how long we'll have with our loved ones and you must live your life to its fullest."

"I understand and I will."

"Then come." She stood and tugged her with her as she did. "This day will be done if we dinnae leave, and you have a very important letter to deliver to your father. He must receive it."

"I can't wait to see my childhood home." She grabbed her riding hat, plunked it on and tied the ribbon under her chin as she wandered downstairs with Zenia.

She would live her life to its fullest as Zenia had implored her to, and as Dad would wish for her to as well.

* * * *

Along with Arianna's letter, James stowed the supplies they needed for the day ahead under his skiff's rear bench seat. Above, the skies were thick with puffy clouds tinged with a little gray. Out in the bay, the waves tumbled in, foamed over the slick rocks and withdrew. 'Twas good weather for sailing, and a good day for wooing the woman he intended to wed. Aye, he just needed to convince Arianna that he'd allow nothing to stand in his way.

"James!" Arianna rushed along the stone landing, her long golden blond tresses streaming behind her and her blue skirts flapping about her legs. She smiled, her lush pouty lips lifting so deliciously.

He bounded out and caught her as she jumped into his arms. He shoved one foot back, barely keeping them both from toppling into the loch. "You're a mischievous imp."

"Just trying to keep you on your toes." She popped a kiss on his cheek. "I missed you and I can't wait to see my old home."

"Then allow me to aid you on board." He handed her into his skiff and once she'd settled at the rear, he offered Zenia a steadying hand.

"Thank you, James." Zenia perched on the seat at the bow and arranged her olive skirts around her. "Do you believe we'll make good time today?"

"'Twill take no more than a half hour to reach the village." They would be sailing in the opposite direction from the day before, heading south and deeper within Loch Dunvegan's inland channel. He released their mooring rope, coiled and stored it then rowed until he cleared the bay. With a gentle wind blowing, he raised the sail, secured the ropes and sat next to Arianna at the stern. He adjusted the rudder, keeping them on course as the hills rose high on his left and the moors rolled away into the distance on the right of the sea's shore.

Zenia pulled the shell she'd collected the day before from her pocket and gazed at it with a soft smile. She pressed it to her heart then slowly sighed and slid it back into her pocket.

Arianna nestled into his side, her face lifted to the sky, a serene and peaceful expression on her face. "Thank you for escorting us today."

"'Tis an honor to bring you both. You'll need to point out the cove you mentioned yesterday where you used to collect shells for your mother." He'd promised her they'd stop on the way.

"The cove is close. Before we make the village there's a sheltered bay surrounded by cliffs and a ledge carved into the sheer rock face that winds upward to the top."

"I know of it. I've passed it a number of times on my way along this channel."

"In the future the locals call the bay Lovers' Leap because of the tale attached to it."

"The bay has no name that I'm aware of. What is the tale?" He turned the rudder and kept them on course.

"It's said a warrior leapt from the cliff-top in anguish after his beloved had fallen into the raging depths below. The two perished right there in the sea." She shuddered. "I hate that tale."

"All tales must be taken with a grain of salt."

"That's exactly what Dad used to say. He and I would often walk along the cliff trail then follow the ledge down to the beach. Of course the ledge has been widened in the future to make traversing it far easier." She snuggled closer, resting her hand on his leg. "I've been thinking too about where to stow Dad's letter. My mother's memorial stone sits right on the edge of the bluff in front of our home. It's a sacred stone and holds a cavity within, one well protected with a strong casing. Dad and I always opened it up once a year to place my mother's shell inside."

"Wait." Zenia gasped as she held up a hand. "You've spoken of your mother's memorial stone afore but no' of a cavity within."

"Does that matter?"

"Aye, it does. I know of that stone. 'Tis called the Fairy Rock." She smiled and clasped her hands. "Oh, I wish you'd told me sooner. There are several lodges along these cliffs, half belonging to Cunninghams and the other half MacLeods, although now I know the Fairy Rock sits afore your childhood home then that means you used to live in Mathew's lodge."

"Who's Mathew?"

"Mathew is Samuel's brother."

"As in Samuel your betrothed?"

"Aye, and I've visited your childhood home in the past. Mathew was the eldest of the two of them by a year and he and Samuel had a tight bond. Afore I left, Mathew wed a MacLeod and they had a son who they named Samuel in honor of his brother."

"That's incredible. Dad told me the story of the sacred stone when I was a child."

"That is a tale told only to a few, those who hold my ability as well as the keepers of the stone. Your father must be one of the keepers, which makes your memorial stone the perfect place to leave your letter. Absolutely perfect." She clapped. "I also used to visit the bay you spoke of. My mother was rather nifty at sailing a skiff. We'd lay out a blanket and a basket of food and swim in the cove. 'Tis a special place and holds fond memories for me. I shouldnae be surprised your father is of Mathew's line. Mathew's father's name was Samuel and his grandfather afore him. 'Tis a time-honored tradition in their family to name a son so. I wish I'd connected everything you've said afore."

"Yes, and I wish I'd known your mother. How'd she learn to sail so well?"

"From her father. He was a fisherman, although he passed away afore I was born." She glanced ahead and smiled. "We're so close. Around the bend is the bay that leads to the cove."

Arianna stood and he grasped her hips and tugged her back down beside him. The water was rougher where it swept into the bay and he didn't need her toppling overboard. With one hand on the rudder, he sailed them toward land, gliding over the white-capped waves.

"I'm so close to home." Arianna jiggled about.

"We'll be there in a moment." Ahead, deep water swirled

and crashed into the cliff-face. He lowered the sail and guided them toward the thin strip of sand to the side. When the hull scraped the sandy sea base, he bounded out into the knee-deep water and with the bow in hand, hauled the skiff half onto the beach.

"We're really here." Arianna scrambled to the bow and he lifted her free and set her on the sand beside him. He tucked a flyaway lock of her hair behind her ear then smoothed his knuckles over her cheek. Such soft skin, and dusted with entrancing freckles.

Zenia clambered onto the dry sand and with her hands on hips, eyed the cliff and the ledge winding upward. "'Tis as beautiful here as I remembered."

"I'll collect my shells. I won't be long." She searched the beach. She selected several shells then climbed onto the boulder wedged against the cliff and jumped onto the ledge.

"Arianna, where are you going?" He nabbed the mooring rope and secured it to a boulder.

"I promise not to go far. I'm just remembering old times." She walked along the ledge then traced something written within the rock face. "Would you look at that." She tapped the rock. "In the future the letters A and Z are etched into the rock, and they're here even now."

"I know the etching you mean." Zenia gasped as she climbed onto the ledge and joined Arianna. "A is for Anna and Z is for Zenia." A wistful smile touched her face. "I'd forgotten this was here."

"You and your mother carved these letters out?"

"Aye. She liked to mark special spots with our initials."

"Well, I always thought A and Z stood for the first and last letter in the alphabet. At least now I know the tru—"

A massive wave rolled in and drenched them. Arianna slipped, grabbed at the cliff's edge but only managed air. She plummeted toward the sea, hit the water and disappeared within its raging depths.

"Arianna!" Zenia fell to her knees on the ledge and searched the depths below. "James, I cannae see her."

"I'll find her." He bounded onto the ledge, ran and dove.

Chapter 6

Contact with the frigid water stole Arianna's breath. She kicked but her thick velvet skirts dragged her down. The crashing waves tossed her about. So deep. She needed to get to the surface.

Her back slammed into the rock wall and knocked the air from her lungs. She'd swum at this cove too many times to count and she could get herself out of this. She shoved away from the cliff and clawed toward the surface. All she had to do was grab a decent breath and swim back to the skiff. Poor Zenia. She'd be so worried, and James, he would certainly blame himself for her fall.

The twisting current tumbled her head over heels and black hazed her vision. Perhaps she'd best get rid of these skirts first. She fumbled for the ties and thumped into the cliff again. Her head hit the rock and black hazed her vision. No. *"Zenia, help me, I need..."* She tried to form the words but her chest burned then a dark void sucked her downward. An unearthly force swept her through the water and tossed her onto the sand. With what strength she had, she flopped onto her back and tried to bring the cliff into focus. Blackened clouds churned high above then a mist swirled and surrounded her. Lightning forked and sizzled in a stunning display of electric whites and yellows then lights shimmered all around, as if the stars themselves had escaped the sky and blazed above.

* * * *

Drenched, James paced the thin strip of sand as the midday sun slipped behind a layer of gloomy gray cloud. Two hours ago, Arianna had fallen into the loch and he'd done naught but search the depths since the moment she had. He stumbled toward Zenia as she sat hunched on the boulder wedged against the ledge, her sobs tearing his heart into pieces. "I cannae find her, Zenia, no' even a body."

"That there is no body is a good thing." She met his gaze, her eyes red-rimmed. "I heard her soul's cry for aid and opened a portal. It all happened so quickly and I had to act fast to give her a chance at survival. She's traveled James, to wherever her light now shines brightest, or she better have. I cannae stand the thought that she may have perished." She thumped her chest. "'Twould kill me. She must live."

"She belongs here with us." This was all his fault. He shouldn't have allowed her to step one foot on that ledge. He collapsed onto his knees in the sand, his heart torn in two.

"We must keep the faith that she lives"—she squeezed her eyes shut then opened them again—"and to see to her last request."

Aye, Samuel Cunningham must receive her letter and heed Arianna's advice. His grief pummeled and drowned him in its intensity.

"There can be no delay." Zenia hurried toward his boat. "We must leave now and store her missive inside her mother's memorial stone."

"Aye, I'm coming." He wouldn't fail Arianna again. He shoved to his feet and raced after Zenia. Arianna was his and had been since the moment she'd arrived in the past. He'd told her he wouldn't suffer a separation from her and he intended to keep that promise. "After we deliver the letter, I'll need your aid, Zenia. I must find a way to get to her."

"You wish to travel through time?"

"Aye, just as we hope Arianna has done." He offered her a steadying hand as she climbed into the boat. "Will you help me?"

"There is great danger in what you ask." She clung to the bow as he pushed the boat into the water and bounded in. "You must be near death, or breathing your last, and if your body remains behind then there is naught more I can do other than to free your soul."

"I gladly accept any danger. I'll do whatever it takes to reach her." He rowed until he cleared the bay then raised the sail.

A mile along the waterway a prominent bluff rose with a two-story lodge built on its flattened peak. Curved windows nestled underneath a steeply thatched roof and a thick forest guarded its back.

"That's Mathew's home." Zenia wrung her hands together. "The village is close, around the next bend."

He sailed alongside the cliffs, past fishermen casting their nets from their boats and into the bay. Longhouses lay spread within the village's basin, and in front of the stables where the grass grew thick, two stable hands brushed down corralled horses.

He guided his skiff over the breakers then jumped into the knee-deep water and hauled the boat up onto the grassy verge. "Pass me my satchel. It holds Arianna's letter."

Zenia tugged it out from under the seat and handed it over.

He slung it over one shoulder then swung her onto dry land and strode toward the stables and the lads. "We're in need of two mounts," he called out.

"Where to, sir?" the one rubbing down a black war horse asked.

"To Mathew Cunningham's lodge on the bluff."

"Mathew passed by here this morn. He rode out to the field beyond the village to watch the foot races. Most of our clansmen are there. Do you still wish to ride to the bluff?"

"We do, and we'll await Mathew there."

"Aye, sir." The lad whistled to the other hand. "Saddle the palfrey for the lady while I ready this destrier." He lugged a brown saddle onto the black stead then tightened the cinch.

James steered Zenia to the palfrey and once the lad had saddled it, he cupped his palms and hoisted her up.

She adjusted her olive skirts, took her horse's reins in hand and motioned with a tip of her head toward the entrance to the forest where three children chased each other in a game of tag. "We need to follow that trail. It leads inland but then veers back toward the sea."

"Aye, we'll ride fast." He tossed the lad a coin and bounded onto his mount. Reins in hand, he slapped them against the horse's neck and bolted, Zenia close behind.

Through the forest opening they rode, autumn and elm trees growing tall either side. He galloped hard. He had no idea how time travel worked, but all his senses fired with the knowledge that every second counted. They had to deliver the letter and as quick as they could.

"Take the trail to your left," Zenia called a half mile along, her long shirts flapping at her ankles. "It heads directly to the lodge."

He veered along the path she motioned to and soon the salty sea air once again teased his nose. Racing, he broke through the heavy tree line. Ahead, the lodge stood at the edge of the bluff, the most welcoming sight. He pulled his horse to a halt next to the hitching post, jumped down and looped his reins over it. "Where's the Fairy Rock?"

"'Tis close. I'll show you the way." Zenia dismounted, tethered her horse next to his and dashed past the bushes to the very edge of the cliff where a six foot high rock, one very similar to a standing stone, stood. "This is her memorial stone."

"And where is the cavity within?"

"I'll show you." The wind blew and whipped her red-gold locks about her face as she knelt in the grass before it. "Have you ever heard the tale of the fairy princess and the MacLeod chief she fell in love with? It would go some way in helping me explain why this rock is so sacred and how the cavity was created."

"Aye, I'm well aware of the tale."

"Good." She pressed her palms against the stone's side. "The son the fairy princess had with the chief, the child she was forced to leave behind had the ability to open a portal between his mother's fairy realm and ours. 'Tis said he traveled often between the two places in time after his tenth year when his ability first came into being. That too is when mine did, as it did for all those who've held my skill as well."

"I see. The princess's son was a lost soul, a child who belonged to two worlds. That's why he could travel."

"Aye. His light shone brightest with both his mother and father, although he traveled without hovering on the edge of death, his fairy blood so very strong. This place, where this stone sits, is where the lad first discovered his gift. When he did, his light pierced the rock he stood beside and created a cavity within."

He knelt beside her and ran his hands over the rough surface while a hundred feet below, the waves pounded into the cliff-face and sent a light spray drifting over them.

"The cavity is here." She traced over a crack in the side, thumped the center then wriggled the edges with her fingers. "Those with the ability to open a portal are always shown this rock and told the tale I've spoken of. Tormod MacLeod, the old chief, brought me here the day after I opened my first portal." She thumped the rock again and dust trickled from the crack. "He is the one who showed me what lies within this rock."

"Allow me to aid you." He continued to work the stone casing loose then grunted as it slid free and exposed the hollow within. The hole was perfect, clean and well protected. "No' only will we leave Arianna's letter here, but I want to leave a missive for her too." He had to let her know of the love he held deep in his heart for her, that he'd never suffer a separation, just as he'd promised.

"I'll go and find some parchment. I willnae be long." She hurried toward the lodge, hauled the back door open and disappeared inside.

He closed his eyes and pressed his palms against the rock. A level of peace flowed over and settled deep inside him. 'Twas as if he could sense Arianna. She was close even though so far away. "I will come for you, Arianna," he whispered. "Wherever you are. I will come."

"Here. I have all we'll need." Zenia rushed back to him and plopped down on her knees in the grass. "I also found a small tin box to store the letters inside." She handed him a wooden board, a piece of parchment and a quill and ink.

He set the parchment on the board, dipped the quill into the ink and scrawled across it. He wrote to the only woman he'd ever love that his greatest desire was for her to live, that Samuel Cunningham would receive the letter she'd written him and survive his illness. Then he told her he would come for her, that she was his, always and forever.

Done, he passed Zenia the parchment and quill.

She wrote after him, tears shimmering in her eyes as she did and once finished, she passed the paper back along with the small tin box.

He scrawled Arianna's name and his own on the outside then from his traveling bag, withdrew the letter she'd written for her father and folded both papers inside the tin. He pressed the lid in place and slid the box inside the cavity.

"There's one more thing I'd like to add." Zenia dug in her

pocket and pulled out the cream fan-shaped shell with its heart of pure white. "'Tis only right I leave this for her." Zenia laid it on top of the box.

Carefully, he eased the stone casing back in place and prayed for a miracle.

* * * *

Pain hammered inside Arianna's head. She forced her eyes open and clutched handfuls of soft sand underneath her. The cliff rose high, the beach and ledge clear of any other. She was still at Lovers' Leap, but where were James and Zenia? She rubbed her dizzy head. She must have lost consciousness. She scrambled to her knees then shoved to her feet and swayed. No, she had to remain alert. A darkened mist swirled and surrounded her. Lightning forked and sizzled and stars shimmered in a brilliant blaze. Not again. She clutched her belly as it rolled, as her scream echoed through the dense fog of nothingness and reverberated in her own ears.

A weightless sensation overwhelmed her and a cold wind whipped her wet blue skirts against her legs. The void sucked her into it once again.

"Careful, Arianna." Hands grabbed her from the dark abyss, hauled her into the bright light of day and away from the edge of a road. "It's too dangerous to cross the road here."

A car whizzed by and tooted its horn and the dance studio's building stood tall, its wooden plaque proudly displaying its name on the sign above the doors.

"Dad?" She swayed and grabbed the man she'd left behind four years ago. "W-where did you come from?" He hadn't aged a day. Actually he looked younger, with less lines around his eyes and his skin no longer so pale. "Am I dead?"

"No, you're alive and I have good news for you."

"What good news?"

"I didn't wish to worry you this morning before your dance practice, but I had an appointment with the doctor and—" He frowned as his gaze moved down her body. "Ah, what are you wearing, love?"

"I, ah,—" This was going to sound farfetched. "You see—"

"Damn. This was the moment it happened, wasn't it?"

"The moment what happened?"

"You're wearing clothing from the fifteen-hundreds, and you're drenched to the skin. Here, take this." He whipped his gray woolen coat off and wrapped it around her shaking shoulders. Cars zoomed by on the black top and a delivery truck beeped as it reversed into the side alley. She truly was home.

Gently, Dad cradled her cheeks in his work-roughened hands and searched her face. "It's clear to see now. You no longer appear seventeen, and from your letter I'd say you're twenty-one. You must have traveled not long after you wrote me."

"Oh my goodness. You got one of my letters? How? When? From whom?"

"From James MacDonald and Zenia MacLeod. Your letter was written on such old parchment and sealed inside a tin box inside the memorial stone's cavity, right where we place your mother's shells. I found your letter when you were very young, the first time I wedged the casing loose. The paper you wrote on was so brittle but I kept it and followed your instructions. You told me not to speak to you about what had happened for fear I'd change your first trip through time, one that had to occur if you were ever to send word to me and save my life. You spoke of Zenia, the Cunninghams, and James."

"You truly got one of my letters?"

"Yes."

"How young was I?"

"A few days at most. They wrote to you as well, James and Zenia. Their letter was inside the box with yours."

"Incredible." She'd done it, actually gotten a letter to her father, or at least James and Zenia had. She wanted to hug them.

"The things you mentioned in your letter, all the dates and events that were important to us so I would know you'd written the truth, had yet to even happen."

"Yet you still believed me?"

"I knew your words were the truth, purely because of what Zenia had written as well and I couldn't take from her what she'd already gifted to me. Precious time with you."

"What do you mean? What precious time had she gifted to you?"

"I mean your entire life. She gifted every one of your first seventeen years to me."

"You're not making any sense."

"I'm sorry, Arianna. I wish I could have told you everything. You spent four years with Zenia and from your letter I could tell not once had either of you ever realized the truth." He wrapped his arms around her, and said, "That is my fault, but no more. I no longer need to keep the facts surrounding your birth from you, or your mother's true identity."

"Tell me what? What have you withheld?"

"I too have traveled through time."

"What?"

"I'll explain everything. Your mother is Zenia."

"H-hold on. You've always told I was named after my mother, that I bear her name. That's Arianna, not Zenia." She swayed and he held her upright. "I don't understand."

"You're aware there's strong fairy magic in your MacLeod line, and usually one in every generation who has the ability to open a portal."

"I wrote to you about that."

"A fact I already knew. As I lay near death on the battlefield at—"

"Wait, what battlefield?"

"The battle where I almost perished, on the Isle of Lewis. I fought there alongside the MacLeods when the MacKenzies took the castle at Stornoway." He guided her to the dance studio's front steps, sat her down and perched next to her. "Allow me to start at the beginning. Zenia was my betrothed. Her chief, Tormod MacLeod, held the same ability as her, and during the battle on Lewis I was dealt a near deadly blow. Tormod saw me fall and he opened a portal and made a wish. With the power of his ancestral fairy blood, he sent me streaking toward the light, on a journey where I would find peace and aid." His voice turned gravely as if he fought his emotions. "I'm not from this time, Arianna, and neither are you."

"B-but—" Her life had been one great big lie.

"Whenever you raised a question about your mother, I kept as close to the truth as I could, but time travel is in a realm all unto itself and you were just a newborn babe when you were first pulled through Zenia's portal and into my arms."

"I can't believe my mother is Zenia MacLeod."

"Zenia and I first met at Dunvegan Castle while I was training amongst the Chief of MacLeod's warriors. One day during sword practice, I didn't move quick enough and suffered a nasty gash. Zenia tended me and stitched my wound. She was so young, only eighteen, yet I was completely drawn to her. She and I were inseparable from that moment on."

"You fell in love?"

"Yes. And before too long I proposed and asked her to be my wife." A silly grin lifted his lips. "She accepted, and I couldn't have been happier."

"Then the call-to-arms came from the MacLeod chief's kin on Lewis. Zenia told me."

"Yes."

Her heartbeat pulsed out of time and she clasped her chest. "Y-you anticipated your wedding night. She fell pregnant and gave birth to a baby girl some months later in the forest. The cord was wrapped around the child's neck. Zenia told me her child died. That's what Zenia has believed all these years, not that her child traveled through time and somehow survived."

"One must be hovering at the edge of death for them to travel. If there is no body left behind, then that is what can happen. Zenia knows that."

"She doesn't know you lived, not with the life-threatening injuries you'd sustained. The same with her baby. How did I survive?"

"The jump through time must have restarted your heart. I'll never forget the day you arrived. I was shocked. You shimmered into view right before my eyes as I readied for bed. You were so tiny and blue, and your scream"—his eyebrows rose—"you wailed as if you'd been slapped. I wrapped you in a fleecy cloth then made a mad dash with you to the store. I grabbed everything off the shelf I could possibly need for a newborn."

"But how'd you know I was yours?"

"You had my blonde hair, a thick tuft of it, and your mother's beautiful blue eyes, and from the moment I held you, I hadn't been able to let you go. I only felt as ease when you were near. The day you arrived, I named you in honor of both Zenia's mother and mine."

"Zenia's mother's name was Anna."

"And my mother's name was Ari."

"Arianna MacLeod Cunningham," she whispered, shaking her head. "I wish you'd told me." How she wished. It would have changed everything, explained why she'd first traveled to Zenia when she'd opened a portal four years ago. Her soul had known Zenia's, just as it had known her father's.

Dad gripped her hands in his. "The day after I named you, I stood before the memorial stone with you in my arms and recalled Zenia's story. She'd told me about the tale of the fairy princess's son and how he was the first to hold the ability of opening a portal. The boy did so at the age of ten, and right before that stone. When Zenia came into her ability at the same age, Tormod brought her to the rock and showed her the cavity. I felt driven to look inside and when I did, I discovered your letter."

"Zenia never knew I was her daughter." She dropped her face into her open palms, her anguish complete. "You never shared the truth with me. Why, in all this time, have you never tried to return to the past?"

"I don't hold the ability to open a portal, and I've never found a MacLeod who can. As the centuries have passed, so too has the ability within the MacLeod line. I also had you and I couldn't risk your life, not when you'd still yet to live it. In the end, I withheld the truth to keep you safe. I also worried greatly about changing your jump through time and your future still yet to unfold."

"Zenia ensured I had a home. She taught me everything I ever needed to know." Overhead, the clouds darkened and a drop of water splashed her nose then another hit her cheek.

"We're about to get wet, and you're already wet enough." He stood and with an arm around her waist, helped her up. "The car's parked on the side of the road."

She squeezed him tight. "I've missed you so much. I never gave up the dream of returning, to spend just one more day with you. When you first pulled me back from the road you said you hadn't wished to worry me this morning before my dance practice. You had an appointment with the doctor. What did he say?"

"Because of your letter I caught my cancer months earlier than I would have. I still had surgery and treatment, but today I learnt I'm cancer free."

"Truly?" Tears flowed down her cheeks. "My letter made a difference?"

"All the difference in the world. I've kept James and Zenia's letter safe for you all these years too. It's at home in my office." He steered her down the street toward his black SUV. From his pocket, he pulled out his keys, opened the passenger door and helped her inside. He closed the door, strode around to the driver's side and eased inside.

He started the engine, pulled out and drove through Dunvegan Village and along the road toward their cliff-top home. "I promise there'll be more secrets between us. I've kept the truth from you for far too long, and now my reason for doing so no longer exists."

"I love you, Dad, and I never want to be parted from you again."

"I love you too, just as I've always loved your mother. Zenia holds my heart and always will. I've never lost the hope of returning to her, of finding a way as you've managed to do." Dad reached across and clasped her hand as he drove. "Tell me more about James."

"He was there that day I first traveled into the past. He and Zenia both saw a vision of my last moments here in the future and together they've watched over me." Cars whizzed past them on the busy main road carved through the forest. "This past week I traveled with Zenia to attend the Highland Games at Dunvegan and James was there."

Dad indicated and slowed the car, turned off the road and bumped along the stony driveway lined with ash and elm trees. Autumn leaves swirled through the air, a rain of glorious yellows and burnt oranges.

She lowered her window and the ocean and its rhythmic crashing reached her on the brisk sea breeze. Ahead, the stone lodge appeared on the flattened headland overlooking Loch Dunvegan. She was finally home.

Dad stopped in the circular drive and together they walked along the crunchy shell path around the house toward the memorial stone near the cliff's edge. Lovers' Leap wasn't visible from here, but it was only a mere mile away and James and her mother were so close, even though so far away.

She knelt before the stone and pressed her palms against the casing wedged tightly over the cavity. She desperately wanted her mother back. Her heart ached, both for the gift of having Dad close, but also for the loss of those she loved. She'd never be able to aid Zenia with her healing, tend and care for those who knocked on her cottage door. Never be held by James, or lie in his arms after he made love to her, to tell him how much she loved him, and to thank him for all that he'd given her.

"What are you thinking?" Dad knelt next to her.

"Of all we've lost. It's so painful being away from them both."

"That's a pain I understand well, one I've had to endure for the longest time." Tears welled in his eyes and he pulled her back into his arms.

"Dad, tell me about what happened after you traveled through time. I want to know it all."

"Things are a little hazy surrounding my initial arrival. Three or four days after I awoke, I found myself in a hospital with tubes and needles sticking out of me. The building I was in wasn't constructed of stone, but metal and glass, and when I stumbled from my bed and stared out the window, I discovered I was standing several stories above the ground. Below, horses and carts had been replaced by metal boxes on wheels, and not only did birds soar through the air, but so too did the most amazing of crafts. Airplanes I soon learned they were called."

"You must have gotten the shock of your life."

"I did. The hospital staff asked me so many questions and I told them I remembered nothing other than where I lived. They sent someone out here to the lodge and returned with Gerald Cunningham, an elderly man who lived on this property at the time. Being kin, Gerald was the one man I trusted with the truth. He aided me when I first arrived and provided all I needed to survive in this time, although he passed from a heart attack just before your first birthday." He braced an elbow on the knee of his gray slacks. "Gerald left this place to me. He was estranged from his family."

"I wish I'd known him. What happened after he passed?"

"I continued to adapt. I formed friendships where I could and even attended evening classes and studied how to speak without the distinctly heavy brogue of my time. I used the skills I had and combined them with the knowledge I gained and before long, I had a thriving business selling my hand-forged weaponry." He covered her hands with his. "You grew, and the day you turned seventeen, I began to worry. You never told me the exact date of your travel, just the year and that it was after a dance practice session. I also never knew if you'd return, but glad I am it was the same day you left. I would never have survived the passing of four years without you."

"We can't allow Zenia and James to deal with the passing of any time either. We need to return to them, both of us, somehow."

"If you're willing, then I'm willing. I've lived without the love of my life for far too long." He touched his heart. "I want Zenia back."

"So do I, and James." She touched her own heart. "I'm more than willing."

****

"I sense Arianna. 'Tis as if she is close." Warmth raced through James's body and wrapped him securely in its heat as he knelt before Arianna's memorial stone. "Do you feel it?"

"I sense her too, just now." Zenia lifted her face to the sky and smiled. "She lives. She truly lives. I believe we've done it, that she's with her father."

Horses' hooves pounded and two warriors rode free of the forest trail. James stood and gripped his sword hilt. The man on the right was clearly William, the scowl on his face no surprise. "It appears we have company."

"That's Mathew with William. 'Tis been some time since I've seen Samuel's brother, but I would never mistake him." She clutched her chest. "William will ask about Arianna. She and I are rarely apart."

"Arianna may be gone, but her secret must remain between only those of us who already hold it."

"Mathew knows of my ability and saw it rise many years ago." She glanced at the rock. "He even knows of this cavity. He was with Samuel when I first showed it to him, just as I've done with you. I need to tell him what we've done, that the letters within must remain where they are for Arianna's father."

"Then we'll speak to William and Mathew." He was out of choices, the need to keep Arianna's secret out of his hands.

William slowed his mount and pulled his horse to a stop, his padded leather war coat donned and claymore belted at his side. Gripping his reins, he eyed Zenia. "The stable lad informed Mathew he had visitors. 'Twas fortunate I was with him when he did. Where's Arianna and why are you here?"

"I, ah—" Zenia darted a look at Samuel's brother and smiled. "Mathew, 'tis wonderful to see you again."

"As it is to see you, Zenia. You've been gone from Skye for far too long." Grinning, he jumped to the ground in a thick buckskin vest and boots, his blond hair flopping forward over his brow. He pulled Zenia into his arms. "William told me you'd come with him and the earl to the Games."

"I needed to return. 'Twas time." She gestured toward James. "Allow me to introduce you to James MacDonald. He's a trusted friend and offered to bring me today."

Mathew nodded at him. "Welcome, James."

"Thank you."

The wind whistled through and dark clouds moved in overhead. Mathew glanced skyward. "It appears a storm is closing in. The weather can change quickly in the isles. Come inside so we might all speak. I'll light the fire and we can warm ourselves." Mathew looped his horse's reins over the hitching post next to their horses then set a hand at Zenia's back and steered her toward the lodge.

William dismounted and planted his feet wide, halting James in his tracks. "Zenia didnae answer my question. Where's Arianna?"

"She came with us as far as the nearby cove." Pain shimmered through him. "I have difficult news to share. Arianna found a way to return to the future and Zenia opened a portal."

"Arianna has gone?" He narrowed his gaze. "Nay, you appear far too calm for such a thing to have happened."

"I speak the truth, William." Calm was the last emotion rolling through him. Arianna was gone, and he wouldn't survive this day if he didn't find a way to get to her.

"You lie. I'll get the truth from Zenia." He stormed into the lodge.

James pressed his forehead against the stone. "I need you, my imp. Wait for me. I will come for you soon. I promise you this."

Chapter 7

Four days later the grandfather clock struck the midnight hour, its twelve dongs ringing loud in Arianna's ears. She rocked in the burgundy padded chair before her father's desk, one hand holding Zenia's shell with its heart of pure white, and the other gripping the letter Zenia and James had written her.

"I see you still can't sleep." Dad strode into the room in khaki pants and a black turtleneck jumper, his thick blond hair a windblown mess. He crouched before the fire, picked up the metal prodder and stoked the embers.

"And I see you've been out wandering the cliffs again."

"For a good reason." He dropped into the burgundy couch under the window and blew out a long breath. "I need to speak to you. We both know the only way either of us have traveled through a portal is in that moment when we're hovering at the edge of death. You were born with the cord around your neck, a car hit you, and you almost drowned."

She sighed. "I have a terrible track record when you say it like that."

"Yes, you do." He leaned forward on the couch. "Tell me more about when you fell into the loch from the cliff, and be as specific as you can."

"Well, I've already told you a rogue wave came out of nowhere." She slid the shell into the front pocket of her black skinny jeans. "My skirts were too heavy and dragged me down, then the waves pummeled me into the rock wall and I hit my head. I called out to Zenia before some kind of unearthly force sent me spinning around. Whatever it was spat me out onto the beach and when I tried to find Zenia and James, they were gone."

"Is that when you lost consciousness?"

"Yes, for a little bit. I'm not sure how much time passed, but when I awoke, I stood up and a darkened mist surrounded me. There was lightning and stars and then you were there, pulling me away out of the dark and back from the road."

"It's as if during the time you were unconsciousness, you sat somewhere in limbo."

"That's what I believe too. Perhaps until the moment when Zenia and James made it here and stowed your letter inside the stone. Or at least that's what I've come up with." She tapped the polished floorboards with one sneakered foot as she eyed James's letter. She'd read what he and Zenia had written a thousand times in the past four days, each word now emblazoned in her memory. Her own letter to Dad sat on the desk and she ran her finger over the faded words. These two letters were the only ones that had ever made it to the future, those she'd left with the earl lost somewhere and somehow over the centuries.

Dad stood and stared out the window at the memorial stone lit a golden hue by the full moon above. "Whenever I can see the Fairy Rock, peace seeps through me. It's as if Zenia is close and her presence surrounding me."

"I feel the same, as if she and James are here."

"Read their letters to me again."

"Of course." She began with James's.

"To the woman who will forever be mine,

Just hours ago you fell from Lovers' Leap and disappeared within the murky depths of the water below. I couldnae save you and Zenia heard your soul's cry for aid. She opened a portal and made a wish for your safe return to your father's arms. Fairy magic brought you to us, and fairy magic has once again taken you away.

I pray you live, that you made it back to the future and your father received your missive and he survived. I meanwhile cannae live, no' without you.

Know that I will come to you.

You are mine, always and forever.

James."

She traced the scrawled slash of his name. "I love him."

"As he loves you." Dad crossed to her and dropped a kiss on the top of her head. "Read Zenia's note as well."

She cleared her throat and said,

"To my beloved Arianna,

All those souls I've aided over time have all traveled to where their light shines brightest. You traveled to me, a most precious gift. Now I pray that the light that led you away from us returns you to your father, safe and well.

I write these words from the Fairy Rock, a stone I also told Samuel and Mathew about. James needs you, just as I need you, and our hearts cry out for you, to have you back with us. From the depths of my soul, I wish that one day we may once again be reunited. I shall forever remain alert.

I love you.

Zenia."

Dad paced his office, from wall to wall. "Zenia said, '*I wish that one day we may once again be reunited. I will forever remain alert.*' Your light shines brightest with both her and me."

"I'm like the fairy princess's son whose parents lived in two different realms." She set the letter down and rubbed her palms on her jeans. "I've traveled to both of you."

"Yes, and now we have to find a way to get us both back to where we belong, to the past, where those we love live." He stopped before her, took her hands in his. "Are you certain you wish to tread the fine line of death again?"

"Yes, because if I don't return to James, he'll come for me and I can't let him do that."

"Good." He opened his desk drawer and pulled out a sheaf of papers. "Earlier today I drew up a new will at my lawyer's office in the village and signed it. I've left this place to Gerald's eldest son even though they were estranged. It seems only right that this property is returned into his kin's hands. This is a copy of what my lawyer holds. You should read it."

She took the papers from him and perused it while he doused the fire. He'd set all in order, ensuring his lawyer saw to his final wishes should he pass. "It's perfect."

"I also arranged for him to come tomorrow at nine." He grabbed a notepad and scribbled a message to his lawyer that she read over his shoulder. It stated simply to set his will in motion, that he would never return. Dad plunked the note on top of his will, dug into his pocket and dropped his keys on top then held out his hand to her. "Now is the time. No more waiting."

"And exactly where are we going to hover on the verge of death or breathe our last?" She gripped his hand and followed him out the door and across the grassy slope.

"Lovers' Leap seems the most fitting place."

The wind whipped her blond hair about her face and plastered her pink hooded sweater to her chest. They trekked alongside the craggy ridge the mile to the cliff, the wind buffeting against them and the sea roaring with white-capped waves below.

As they reached the ledge that led down to the cove,

thunder boomed in the blackened skies overhead. She shivered and stopped next to Dad.

"I'll go first." He shuffled onto the ledge and once assured of his footing, nodded for her to join him. "Stay close, one step behind me, no more."

She seized the first groove in the craggy rock wall illuminated by the moonlight and stepped down beside him. Far below, the waves crashed into the wall and sprayed high. She shoved one foot in front of the other and shuffled down the path in his wake.

Twenty feet from the bottom, Dad stopped and laid a hand on her shoulder. "This is far enough. We want to arrive in the past breathing our last, but without life-threatening injuries."

"I can't believe we're going to jump from this cliff." Hot tears pricked her eyes. "I love you, Dad."

"I love you too. It's time. Let's do this together." He took one step forward and teetered on the slick edge in his black leather lace-up shoes, the ones she'd brought for him for his last birthday. Hopefully he'd celebrate another birthday this year, and so would she.

"What's the drill once we jump?" She wriggled up beside him.

"We don't fight the water's pull but hold onto each other." He gripped her hand, his voice almost lost to her as the wind rushed around them. "And we call out to Zenia, with everything within us. We'll wish for our safe return to the past."

"Don't let go of me."

"Never." He wrapped his arms fully around her and with his gaze on hers, took her with him as he fell forward into the dark abyss.

* * * *

Lightning slashed the skies and the rain fell. On his knees before the Fairy Rock, pain slammed through James's chest. 'Twas as if someone had taken a sword and thrust it right through his heart. He gasped for breath and the pain slowly receded, but not the sheer ache of longing in his soul for the woman he loved.

"James!" Zenia raced from the lodge, rain streaming down her face and plastering her red-gold curls to her head. She tossed her drenched lacy white shawl onto the ground and clasped his shoulder. "We need to go. It's Arianna. I heard her cry for aid, and another too. Samuel calls to me."

"Samuel? How is that possible?"

"'Tis impossible, although it has happened all the same. We must hurry."

"Where too?" He snagged his horse from its tethered post.

"Where Arianna fell only a few short hours ago. There's no time to lose."

He hoisted Zenia onto his mount and bounded in behind her. Knees thrust into the animal's flanks, he slapped the reins against its neck and tore along the cliff-top trail.

The storm raged, the turbulent black clouds overhead swirling and seething. He urged his black destrier faster along the narrow path. Pine trees swayed on his right and branches scraped his arm while on his left, the sea roared and his horse scattered stones on the verge that clacked down the rock face before disappearing into the watery depths below.

"Faster, James." Zenia clawed his shoulders from behind.

"We're almost there," he bellowed over the fury of the storm. He rode hard then hauled his horse to a stop where the ledge began.

"I'm here," Zenia cried, her arms lifted skyward. "With the power of my ancestral MacLeod fairy blood, I wish for a portal to open. Free these displaced souls in need of aid and allow them to seek the light. Bring Arianna and Samuel home. Bring them to me."

The earth shook and stars blazed in the churning water far below, a brilliant kaleidoscope of sizzling yellows and whites.

Hell. He had to get to Arianna now.

He bounded from his horse, set Zenia safely on her feet and tore down the ledge. Stars churned within a swirling vortex, and halfway down, he dove, right into the heart of the portal. *"I'm coming, Arianna,"* he called, from his heart to hers.

An unearthly force sucked him down, one he had no intention of fighting as it took him.

* * * *

Arianna drifted within the murky water, Dad's grip on her as tight as hers on him. Never would she let him go. *"I need you, Zenia,"* she cried out. *"Please, don't forsake me now. I want to come home to you and James."*

Lights blazed and shimmered all around, beautiful yet so deadly as she forced herself to stay focused. Words drifted through her mind, the sweet sound that of James's voice, *"I'm coming, Arianna."*

Arms clamped around her waist and she jerked around and stared into the most piercing blue eyes. James firmed his hold on her and Dad and pushed them upward through the swirling depths, and in a flurry of bubbles, they broke the surface. Lightning crackled overhead and waves pounded into her.

She gulped in great drafts of air. "J-James? Is it really you?"

"Aye. You left me and you'll never do so again." He cupped the back of her head and drew her closer. His auburn hair floated around his neck as he glanced at her father.

Dad slugged in air, fog pulsing from his mouth in the icy cold as he did. "We made it, Arianna."

"We did." She wrapped one arm around his neck and hugged him hard while she still held onto James.

"Samuel!" Zenia scrambled down the ledge then jumped onto the beach.

"Wait there, Zenia!"

"Is it really you?" She clasped one hand over her mouth and

the other over her heart.

"Yes, my love." He blew her a kiss. "I'm coming."

"Arianna!" she cried, her face so pale. "No more falling from this cliff. My heart cannae take losing you again. Come here now. I need to hold you."

Dad and James both kicked her toward the beach.

At hip-depth, James swept her up and carried her to Zenia and set her on her feet.

Zenia hauled her into her arms and hot tears streamed down their mashed cheeks and flowed together. "I've never known such agony and joy as I have this day."

"Zenia." Dad wrapped his arms around them both and they all clung to each other. "Every single day I've been gone, I've longed to return to you."

"How are you alive?" She clasped his cheeks in her hands.

"At the battle on Lewis, Tormod MacLeod sent me through a portal toward the light. That light led to the future, to a time when incredible medical advances ensured my survival, although I've never been able to return even though I desperately wished to."

"Tormod told me of the portal he opened, but I never once considered you lived even though your body was gone, no' with the injuries he spoke of."

"I lived." He grinned and twirled her around. "I can't believe I have you back. I love you."

"I love you too." She giggled, her face raised to the sky. "I have my beloved back."

Arianna laughed and jumped into James's open arms. "Dad and I have so much to tell you both."

"Start wherever you wish." He stroked her back and rained kisses down on the top of her head.

"First, let me introduce you to my dad. James, this is my father, Samuel Cunningham. Dad, this is James MacDonald." She grasped Zenia's hand and said to her, "After my return to the future, I learnt the baby you had with Samuel twenty-one years ago, was in fact me."

"Oh my." Zenia's face paled and her knees buckled. Dad scooped her up then held her against his chest. Zenia looked into his eyes. "I was so overwhelmed by yours and Arianna's return I had no' yet been able to think beyond that. How did our child survive, and come to be with you?"

"You believed you'd lost her in childbirth and opened a portal to set her free. She traveled to me, although something happened during that trip through time because her heart restarted. She arrived right before my eyes with a very loud wail."

"You've cared for our daughter all this time?" Zenia stroked Dad's cheek. "'Tis astonishing."

"Yes, as you've cared for her these past four years. I'm so sorry. I withheld the truth from Arianna because I believed that to be the right thing. I also told her I'd named her after her mother. She never knew the truth. Can you forgive me?"

"You did what you thought best and I can accept that. Arianna lives because of you."

"She also lives because of you." He kissed her and carried her to the ledge, the two speaking quietly as they left.

James wrapped Arianna tightly in his arms. "I didnae even know Zenia had given birth to a child."

"Neither did I until the morning before we set sail for the village. She told me the first time then, not that I would have guessed she was my mother even after I heard her story. Zenia lived in the past and as far as I was aware I'd been born in the future to a woman named Arianna. When Dad told me the truth I was shocked."

"How do you feel now?" His gaze roamed her body.

"Wonderful, like I'm living again. I've missed you so much. These past four days have been so difficult."

"Four days?" Confusion burned deep in his midnight blue

eyes. "You fell from Lovers' Leap only this morn, four hours ago."

"Really? Oh, then it appears time truly has no meaning when one travels through a portal. When I arrived in the future, it was at the same moment when I first left. Dad pulled me back from the road and after he did, he told me about the letter he'd received from me, one you'd left inside the stone. He found those letters not long after I was born."

"Zenia and I delivered them as soon as we could. We sensed the urgency." He looked deep into her eyes, covered her mouth with his and kissed her with fierce passion. Heat radiated from every place where they touched and she pushed her fingers deep into his thick hair and held onto him.

"You're making me hot," she whispered against his lips. "And that's not an easy feat to do when I'm drenched to the skin."

"I cannae leave this place until I've asked you one very important thing." He lowered to one knee, a deep look of longing in his eyes. "Arianna MacLeod Cunningham, I cannae live on this Earth without you. I love you, endlessly, and I wish to take you as my wife, to bind you to me for all time. Will you do me the great honor of marrying me?"

She clasped his face and squealed. "Yes, yes, yes. You're mine, James MacDonald, and I can't wait to be your wife, always and forever."

"You'll never leave me again." He kissed her, ravenously, and she kissed him as wildly in return.

No, she'd never leave him again.

He was hers, her beacon of light and her greatest desire, for all time.

Chapter 8

The rain eased and stopped as they climbed the ledge and made it to safety at the top of the cliff. "I'm so excited to be back." Arianna twirled around and James caught her and held her close.

Horses' hooves pounded and shook the ground and James withdrew his sword. "Riders approach."

Dad moved and stood shoulder to shoulder with him as William and Mathew burst out of the forest and pulled their horses to a stop.

"Mathew." Dad gasped then jogged toward the men.

"Is that Dad's brother?" Arianna gripped Zenia's hand. The man had blond hair and Dad's narrow nose and deep cleft in his chin. They looked so similar.

"Aye, that's Mathew Cunningham, your uncle."

A grin slashed Mathew's face and he grasped Dad's arms. "Samuel? How are you alive?"

"It's a long story and one I'll gladly explain."

William bounded across to Arianna. "I was told you'd fallen from the cliffs here and returned to the future."

"I did, and now I've returned with my father."

"'Tis astonishing." He glanced between her and her father.

"How do Mathew and your father know each other?"

"You need to catch my father's long story. For now, I have good news to share. James proposed." Such joy burst through her. "And I said yes."

"Nay." He groaned and glared at James.

"Please, be happy for me, William. You two have never seen eye to eye, but I love him."

"I dinnae care for a MacDonald becoming kin."

"You've no choice." James tucked her under his shoulder then extended his hand to William. "I can let bygones be bygones if you can."

"I cannae believe I must shake your hand." William snorted but still did. "For Arianna's sake, just ensure you care for her well. If you dinnae, I'll gladly take your head off."

"You can be assured I'll care for her as if my very life depended on it." James smiled at her then kissed the tip of her nose. "Would you still like to visit your childhood home? We never did quite get there."

"Yes, please." She shivered. "And to get out of these wet clothes."

James whistled for his horse and it clomped out from within the heavy tree line. He hoisted her onto his mount, slid in behind her and banded his arms around her tight.

Mathew offered Dad and Zenia his horse, then doubled up with William on his destrier. They rode side by side, Dad telling Mathew and William all.

When they reached the clearing next to the lodge, Arianna's breath caught, her heart tugging at the glorious sight. The lodge was so close to what she'd known in the future, right down to the shell pathway around the side of the house. The forest guarded its back and the memorial stone took pride of place at the cliff's edge. "It looks just like home." She snuggled back against James. "Or I should say my old home."

"Aye, you should. Your new home will be with me." James

jumped to the ground and swept her down beside him. With one finger under her chin, he tipped her face up and looked into her eyes. "Having you at my side is all I long for."

"I was so worried you'd try to travel through time to find me."

"I would have. You'll never leave my side again, or risk your life as you have this day. Do we have an understanding?"

"We do. I need you, and I don't want to live without you ever again either."

Mathew beckoned them inside. "Come, everyone. Out of the cold."

"Let's go." James hitched his horse to the post then steered her toward the front door after her parents.

"Where is your wife?" Dad asked Mathew.

"She and my son, Samuel, are away visiting her kin. They're due back at the end of the week." Mathew led the way down the hallway and gestured toward the far chamber. "Arianna, take the chamber overlooking the cliffs. It has a tub and I'll bring you some hot water so you may bathe and warm yourself."

"Thank you."

James ushered her down the hallway and into the very room that had been hers in the future.

Soaking wet, she dripped water on the polished wooden floorboards as she crossed to the four-poster bed. She perched on the end, unlaced her black and pink Nike sneakers then rose and propped them before the hearth.

"I'll get a fire started." He knelt at the fireplace and pulled stringy dried bark from a log and over it, struck a small piece of flint with his dirk. Breathing on the sparks, he coaxed them to life then added wood and brought the fire to a crackling blaze.

"Here's the water." Her uncle returned with pails in hand, William right behind him carrying water as well. They filled the tub then Mathew closed the door behind them as he and William left.

"You're shivering something fierce." James unfolded the wooden clothes rack and placed it before the fire. "Lay your wet clothes here to dry."

"Thank you." She hauled her pink sweater over her head and draped it over the rack.

James gazed at her as she unbuttoned her long-sleeved white blouse. "What is that you're wearing underneath?"

"It's called a bra." She tossed her blouse on the rack and sashayed toward him, her nipples poking the wet white silk.

"It's rather transparent." He lowered to his knees, planted his hands on her waist and eyed her black skinny jeans. "And these appear to be plastered to your skin."

"They're called jeans and now they're wet, they'll be hard to get off."

"Where do I start?"

"With the domes at the front. You release each one." She pushed her fingers deep into his thick auburn hair and held onto him. "Every night for the past four days I've dreamed of you."

"I could no' have lived through four days without you. Four hours was a lifetime." He fiddled with the domes on her jeans until he snapped each one open. He shimmied the black denim down her legs, tugged it over her ankles as she raised each foot and tossed them onto the rack. He licked his lips, his gaze on her matching white silk panties. "Sweet heaven. You must wear such underclothing again."

"I will, but for now, they need to go." She guided his hands to the waistband of her panties. "These go down, and my bra unclips at the back."

He peeled her panties down her legs, palms warm on her skin as he stroked downward. "I need to love you, as I did last eve."

"I need that too."

"A good answer." His voice was a purr as he kissed her

belly then licked the skin along her inner thighs. He skimmed his warm hands over her calves then slowly trailed them up as he rose. Heat raced along the path he touched, behind her knees and over her outer thighs. Behind her, he puffed hotly against her bare skin as he removed her bra. "Hop in the tub."

"Only if you join me."

"I would never turn down such a request." His voice cracked as his gaze roamed her body.

"Then you need undressing too." She sidled against him, tugged his damp tunic from his pants and lifted it over his head before dropping it onto the floor.

He kicked off his boots and removed his sword. Such a deep need burned in his striking blue eyes. "You're so beautiful." His gaze consumed every inch of her. "I want to touch and taste." He cupped her breasts, eased them together then licked one nipple. The raspy stroke of his tongue sent a bolt of pleasure rippling through her core.

"I love how you touch me."

He grinned then swirled around the tip. "You taste divine, and I intend to enjoy my fill of you." He sucked her nipple deep into his mouth and her knees buckled. He swept her up then lowered her into the tub. The warm water cascaded over her skin, adding more heat to the fire already racing through her blood.

"Come in." She clutched his belt and tugged it free of his pants. His muscled shoulders, so broad and strong, bulged as he leaned over her. Every inch of him was so finely honed from hours of sword practice, and his abs rippled, one glorious layer over another. She traced each defined contour and along the delicious tease of auburn hair narrowing down his rigid belly where it disappeared into his pants. Ogling him was a pleasure all unto itself, and touching him, even more so. All she desired was him. "I can't believe you're all mine again."

"Aye, as you're all mine." He loosened the ties of his pants, shoved the dark leather down his thickly muscled legs and off. His cock, thick and flushed a deep plum color at the head, brushed his belly.

She squirmed back to make room for him, and he stepped in and eased down, sloshing water over her chest.

Gaze smoldering, he nabbed the soap from beside the tub and lathered it. "Lean back and relax while I clean you."

"Just make sure you don't miss a spot."

"I'll ensure it." He lifted her feet and placed them against his chest then with the thick mound of bubbles, massaged her heel, her high arch and around her toes. He did the same with her other foot, his thumbs kneading with delicious strokes as she rested her head against the rim.

"I also wish to speak vows afore this week is done." He brushed her hair away from her breasts where it swirled then rubbed his thumbs over her nipples. They beaded and a fiery tingle radiated outward from the tips.

"Yes, please."

"You've become rather agreeable all of a sudden." He stroked her calves then worked upward and hands on her thighs, dragged her closer, his legs underneath her body as he kept her afloat over him. "'Tis rather pleasing that you have, and now I give you fair warning. Since I have the bounty of my dreams afore me, I intend to gorge." He lifted her legs over his shoulders and brought her right up against him. Gently, he dipped his finger along her folds then rubbed her clit.

"Gorging is good." She moaned and squeezed her eyes shut. "Oooh, very good."

"Nay, look at me, Arianna. I need to see your pleasure when it comes."

"Everything you do brings me pleasure." She looked into his eyes as he plunged one finger deep inside her. She bucked as he stroked, so hard and fast until he curled his finger into a spot that had her arching out of the water. "Oh, I won't be able to hold on if you keep doing that."

"Then come as you please."

"No, only with you." Her heartbeat pulsed out of rhythm and she reached underneath her, caressed the hard length of his erection and allowed the memory of their last night together to consume her. Matching him stroke for stroke, she fondled him in long pulls.

He groaned, long and low and the wickedly decadent sound sent a blaze of desire flaring through her.

"I need more of you." Ragged words as he lifted her bottom higher, brought her entrance to his mouth and sucked her clit, hard. She came, her core rippling with wave after wave of pure pleasure and before she could descend he released her legs and with one arm around her waist, lifted and impaled her on top of him. He took her mouth in a hot kiss, gripped her hips and moved her up and down over his hard cock.

Another orgasm built, so quickly following the first that they ran one straight into the other. Faster, she needed to move faster. He'd taken her over and yet she still wanted more. She gasped as her channel tightened and pulled him in all the way to his balls. "Yesss."

"I'm right here with you."

"Always with me, my champion." She cried out as a bright array of sizzling colors burst behind her closed eyelids and she flew, pulsing around him and dragging him home.

Never would she let him go again.

He was hers, and would be for all time.

* * * *

James shuddered as Arianna came around his cock. He could no longer hold the sensations storming through his body back. His thoughts flew and his release burst from in a steady stream. Within the woman he loved, he spilled his seed deep.

Slowly, he came back down and rested his head against the edge of the tub, his hands firm around her waist.

"I love you." She nuzzled his neck, drew his skin deep inside her mouth and sucked. "I believe we should try out the bed."

"Did I no' sate you?" He dipped one finger through her curls and caressed her clit.

"Yes, but I might be a little demanding for a few days."

"Then to the bed we go." He rose and carried her out of the tub and to the bed. With their wet bodies sliding together, he laid her down on the soft furs and took her mouth in a ravenous kiss.

He'd longed for her every moment of their separation, to have her back in his arms and to join with her and make her his in every way. Kissing her, tasting the delectable recesses of her mouth had his cock rising and throbbing once again for release. He'd take all she offered and demand even more.

Tracing her skin with his mouth and tongue, he slid down her body. He lapped at her full breasts and imbibed on her pebbled nipples until she cried out his name. He feasted on her creamy flesh then glided down to her entrance and blood pounding, lowered his head to her clit and razzed the tip with his teeth. "My woman. I will always love you."

"James. Need you. Now." She thrashed her head from side to side.

"As I need you." With his hands on her hips, he pressed his cock to her wet folds and plunged inside her.

Pleasure overflowed him and with his body buried deep inside her, he forged the timeless connection between them that he would endlessly crave. Aye, now he'd claimed his woman and his future, she would forever be his.

Chapter 9

Standing high on the grassy hills surrounding Dunscaith Castle a month later, Arianna rested back against her warrior champion, his arms wrapped tight about her waist and his fingers threaded through hers over the slight bump of her belly, a child she'd yet to tell him about. James had brought her to his home and as promised he'd wed her within the week, surrounded by his clansmen and her family. She'd never been so happy or so excited as her parents too had spoken their vows the following day.

"Look." James pointed toward the training yard near the shore where a good amount of flat land sat on the edge of the loch. A cloud of dust rose from the warriors hard at sword practice. "Your father battles my brother. Alex is struggling to gain an upper-hand."

"Dad always competed in the local Games. He didn't just forge weapons of old, but trained with them as well."

Zenia stood watching him from the edge of the training yard with a wide smile, her basket of herbs looped over her arm and her red-gold curls glimmering in the late afternoon sunshine. Her parents had found a plot of land close by and after the winter would begin building a new home.

James's mother, Mary, strolled toward Zenia, her own basket overflowing with wildflowers. She stopped and the two spoke. Mary had accepted and welcomed them all to Dunscaith, and she couldn't have asked for a more wonderful and loving new clan.

Beyond the training yard, the waters of Loch Eishort shimmered blue-green from this vantage point and children played near the stables, their giggles reaching her on the brisk sea breeze. Overhead, the sun shone and wispy clouds dotted the horizon, floating toward the Cuillin mountains. Beyond the hilly range sat Dunvegan, her uncle only a mere day or two's sail away. They would visit with him again soon. She smiled at the thought. This was her true place in time and she was finally home.

"I think 'tis time." James rubbed his chin over the top of her head, his warmth fully surrounding her.

"Time for what?"

"For my next surprise."

"I love your surprises." She turned in his arms and faced him. Every day he'd shown her another place that intrigued her, from hidden caves to gloriously secluded lochs where they'd swum then relaxed on the mossy bank as the sun had warmed their bare bodies.

"This place is very special. It's on my land and close to where we'll build our own home when the time comes." Holding her hand, his fingers tangled with hers, he guided her over the rise and along the grassy track scattered with rocks. They walked through a field of heather then down toward the ocean. Waves rushed into shore and foamed over the pebbly beach.

They continued on, around the loch's tip until they stopped before a massive rock wall with trailing ivy. James brushed aside a clump of the thick foliage and edged through a thin gap.

"Where are we going?" She followed in his tracks and scampered along a wet tunnel carved of stone. "What is this place?"

"We're almost there. Look." He emerged into a beam of sunshine.

"Oh my. This is beautiful." She pressed her hand to her chest. A secluded cove with a thin strip of golden sand sat before her, and on either side of the beach, the cliffs rose high. "This reminds me of Lovers' Leap. It's so private."

"Very private, and all ours." He unbelted his plaid, flapped it out and laid it on the sand.

A gentle breeze whispered around them, lifted his shirt hem and gave a glimpse of his golden skin. His tan leather pants hung low on his hips and clung to his powerful thighs. He removed his sword and weapons, lifted his white tunic over his head and tossed it onto his tartan then prowled toward her. "Do you wish to swim?"

"A swim sounds wonderful."

"Then allow me to aid you with these laces." He picked up the front ties of her sapphire gown and unlaced her stays, his warm breath feathering across every inch of skin he exposed. Slowly, gently, he slid the fabric covering her shoulders down her arms and over her hips. The velvet swished into a puddle at her feet and exposed all of her.

"Now it's my turn to aid you." She loosened his pants ties, and he kicked off his boots and shoved the leather down his legs and off.

"You have the most gorgeous hair, Arianna. It glimmers like gold in the sunlight." He played his fingers through her blond tresses then scooped her into his arms and walked into the water, his erect shaft brushing her bare bottom. In he strode until he reached his waist, his hungry gaze making her catch her breath.

"You say the most wonderful things." She caught his face in her hands and brought his mouth to hers. She kissed him and he kissed her back with such heated passion. Every inch of her throbbed and burned for more. "I have a surprise for you too, one I intend to share before you make me forget."

"And what would that be?"

"You're going to be a daddy."

"What?"

"We're going to have a baby all of our own."

He whooped and twirled her around then gently set her down on her feet and caressed her belly, holding her and their child close. "I promise you my unending devotion. There is none I love and desire more than you."

"And I promise you forever." She reached up onto her toes and whispered against his lips. "I wish to soar to the stars."

With dedicated devotion he joined them together and sent them both flying skyward.

Their love had bloomed and taken hold from the very beginning. He was the man she'd traveled through time to, and the man who would forever be hers.

To fairy magic and wishes made from the soul. May they always come true.

Author's Note

This story is set in the year fifteen-hundred and ninety at a time when the blood feuds ran rampant between the Highlander clans of the Western Isles of Scotland.

During this period, the king had imprisoned the three chiefs, Lachlan MacLean of Duart, Donald MacDonald of Sleat, and Angus MacDonald of Dunnyveg. He intended to bring a halt to the feud and for them to atone for their actions, and so as each chief arrived in Edinburgh at the king's request, they were apprehended and imprisoned. In the first five stand-alone books in this Highlander Heat series, you can catch the individual stories of the clans, and discover how the feud began and the ramifications of it as it raged.

Donald Gorme Mor MacDonald of Sleat, was the Chief of Clan MacDonald, and with his successor being his nephew Donald MacDonald, a minor at the time, I chose James and his brother to lead the clan.

James MacDonald and Arianna MacLeod Cunningham are fictional characters.

Sir Roderick Ruairidh Mor MacLeod, the fifteenth Chief of Clan MacLeod, was known as Rory, and Margaret was his younger sister.

The Fairy Flag belonging to clan MacLeod does hang within a frame in the great hall of Dunvegan Castle, although it's now merely a thin piece of fabric.

The seventh Earl of Glencairn's eldest son was named William, a young man who would have in fact been fifteen at the time this story was set. The Earl of Glencairn's sister, as stated in this story, was married to the Chief of MacLean which pitted the Cunningham clan against the MacDonalds of Skye in the war that raged at that time.

This story is woven with as much accuracy to the period and locations as possible, but any mistakes made are mine alone.

This book forms part of my *Highlander Heat* series, and each within it are stand-alone.

Please feel free to search for any of my other works. I simply adore strong heroines, and have a ton of fun matching them with their honorable alpha heroes.

Also available in paperback
Scottish Historical Romance

Traveling through time…for a Highlander.

Highlander Heat Series

Highlander's Castle, Book One

Highlander's Magic, Book Two

Highlander's Charm, Book Three

Highlander's Guardian, Book Four

Highlander's Faerie, Book Five

Highlander's Champion, Book Six

by Joanne Wadsworth

Looking for more sexy Scottish adventure?

Read on to catch a preview of the first book in
The Matheson Brothers series.

Highlander's Desire

The Matheson Brothers Book One

by Joanne Wadsworth

Highlander's Desire

The Matheson Brothers Series, Book One

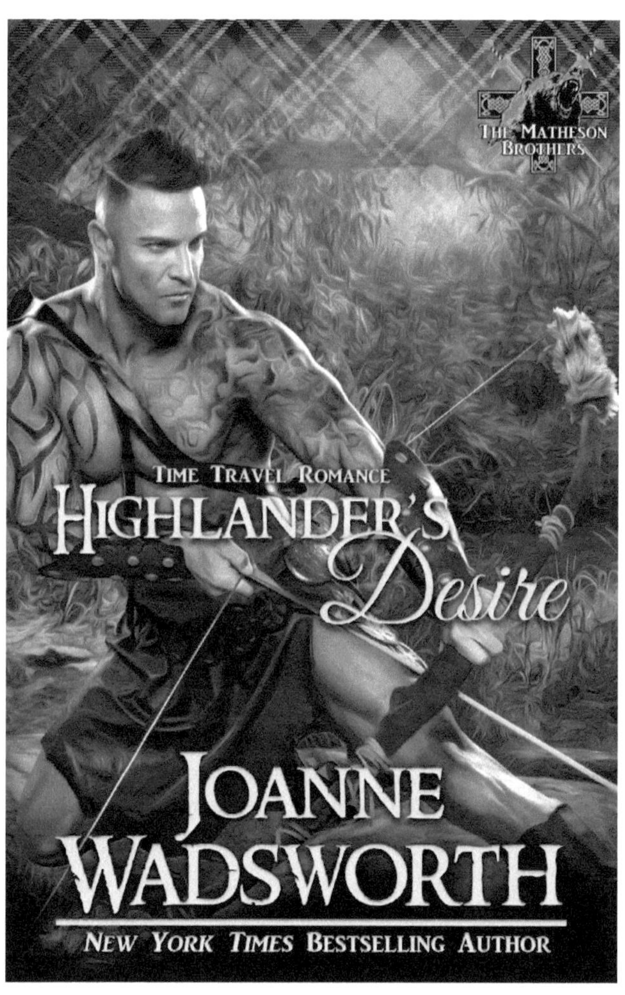

The Prophecy

The ancient House of Clan Matheson, Scotland, 1190.

Sorcha screamed as pain gripped her belly and racked through her.

"Your twin bairns wish to be born, my dear." Nessa, Sorcha's mother and their clan's fae-blooded seer, knelt at her bedside. "I see a vision of them. Two lads of mayhap eight or nine. They're very strong."

"What else do ye see?" Panting, Sorcha fisted the bed sheet either side of her.

"They're tussling and giggling in a meadow as Gilleoin watches on." Nessa caught her hand. "Your sons are so very like their father. They can shift shape, call forth their inner bear, and draw claws."

"Are ye certain?" She longed to give her husband bairns who held his revered ability, one gifted to him by The Most High One. Gilleoin was the first and only known man to hold shifter blood. The night she'd first met him, five years past, had been when he'd sailed along the loch to her village, strode right toward her and gazing into her eyes, lowered to one knee. He'd declared, under the brilliance of the full moon, that a mated bond had formed between them and she was his. She'd sensed the bond too, to the depths of her soul, with her sudden need to touch him and the pure aura of energy surrounding him. Some of her village people, those directly descended from the faerie prince who'd wed their chief's daughter two centuries past, held a touch of fae blood and as such also held rare and divine skills. Upon her birth, she'd received the ability of aura reading and could perceive another's true intentions. Gilleoin's aura drew her toward him and later that night when she'd lain with him, he'd merged their minds with his shifter ability and forged a link along a pathway known only to them. His shifter blood was strong, and though he held not a touch of fae blood and wasn't one of her people, he was still hers and always would be so.

"Very certain, and there's more." Swaying, Mother closed her eyes, her red locks wisped with gray coiled high upon her head. "Your eldest son and his descendants shall possess the skills of our fae people, although your youngest son willnae. He and his progeny shall be shifter alone."

"What skill will my eldest be gifted with?"

"That of death-warning. Of those who live but are soon to die, he shall receive a vision and with his skill save those who perish unjustly afore their time."

"A worthy skill, one Grandfather had. Will my sons seek the ones they're mated too when they come of age, as Gilleoin did with me?"

"Aye, that alone is in their shifter blood, as is the ability to merge minds with the one their soul cries out for. When your sons reach the age of twenty, their soul shall lead them to their mate, the full moon guiding them to their chosen one. To join in all ways, they will need to complete the bond and forge the unbreakable merge of the mind as Gilleoin did with you."

Such relief rolled through Sorcha. "Where shall they find their mates?"

"Your eldest shall remain here, his chosen one from our

village along the loch. She, like you and I, is part fae. She will bear him many bairns, and with the infusion of her fae blood into your eldest son's line, 'twill also ensure our people's fae skills will remain strong in his offspring. Your youngest son though will travel far from this place in search of his chosen one. When he finds her, they will join and their line shall be shifter alone. Your youngest son will grow from strength to strength as chief of his own clan, a mighty leader who will draw the respect of all his people." Nessa stroked her forehead and pushed back her damp hair. "'Tis time for you to push, my dear. Your bairns cannae wait any longer."

"Nay. I must wait for Gill—" Pain surged through her and she cried out and bore down.

She pushed with all that was within her. At the end of the bed, her midwife crouched between her legs and caught her firstborn son as he slid free from her body. The babe let out a mighty cry as her midwife handed her son into her mother's waiting arms.

Nessa carried her grandson to the wide basin on top of the side table, settled him within the warm water and bathed him. Then carefully, she marked the side of her firstborn's neck and wiped the blood from the mark, one which took the shape of a bear's claw ringed by a star. "This claw-and-star mark," her mother said, "will symbolize your firstborn's dual shifter-fae blood."

"A worthy mark for the 'Son of the Bear.'"

"Aye, it is. What shall you name him?" Mother wrapped her crying babe in Gilleoin's Matheson plaid and with him swaddled in her arms, carried him to her.

She held her son and cupped his precious cheek as he gazed at her with striking golden eyes. His aura shimmered so profoundly, the most glorious pure white threaded with heavenly strands of gold. "I shall name him Kenneth, for he carries the divine skills of our fae people in his blood, just as his descendants will do." Each strand of gold in his aura gave proof his progeny would be strongly fae-skilled shifters, just as Mother had said.

"A most worthy name." Nessa took Kenneth from her, kissed his forehead and whispered to him, "You've also been given your late grandfather's name, and he would be honored if he knew." A soft expression crossed Mother's face as she glanced at her. "My dear, 'tis time to push again. Your second son desires to join his brother. The two dinnae care to be parted."

More pain. Her belly tightened and she thrust her elbows into the mattress, bore down and pushed. Her second son wailed with a hearty cry as he emerged and the midwife lifted him up for her to see. Fair hair, just like his elder brother had. So too he had the most stunning golden eyes—shifter eyes. His aura, so pure and white held a tinge of sizzling red around the edges, just as Gilleoin's did. Aye, he was shifter alone and so too his descendants would be. "I shall call him Ivan, for he shall be gifted with strength and wisdom. He shall become a man of great honor when he is called to lead his own clan."

Mother returned Kenneth to the crook of Sorcha's right arm then took Ivan from the midwife and bathed him.

"I shall mark your youngest son as well, but only with the bear's claw to symbolize his shifter blood alone. This mark will grace his line." Gently, she marked the side of her second-born son's neck and wiped the blood away. The singular bear's claw was perfect. Nessa wrapped him in a plaid and rocked him in her arms then carefully settled Ivan within Sorcha's other arm.

Sorcha cradled her sons to her chest, right next to her heart, where they would forever remain. "I've longed for this day, when I would hold you both in my arms. I love ye, as greatly as I love your father."

Mother's eyes filled with tears and one trickled free. "My dear, I must impart to you all I've seen, and you must ensure your sons never forget the prophecy I'm about to speak of."

Nessa's aura shimmered like that of sparkling stars, reflecting her divine honesty and her great seer ability.

"Speak of what you've seen. I will hear it all." Her mother's prophecies, so strong and true, were never to be taken lightly. She would hold whatever words were spoken close to her.

Hands lifted high, Nessa's wise eyes clouded over. *"Gilleoin's sons will separate when they come of age and rule their own clans, yet there will come a time far in the future when a mated bond forms between the two clans. Only then must Gilleoin's descendants once again merge, and the 'power of three' be unveiled."* She opened her eyes and blinked the haze away.

"Why must their descendants once again merge?" Sorcha brushed a kiss over Kenneth and Ivan's brows.

"If they dinnae, then both Kenneth and Ivan's lines shall be like the leaves that fall from the trees. They will scatter too far and wide then turn to dust, and in doing so, their shifter race will be no more."

"Sorcha!" Gilleoin rushed into her chamber, shirttails fluttering over his kilt and his claymore bobbing within the baldric holstered across his broadly muscled back. He stumbled to her bedside, his golden eyes wide. "My love, you've birthed our bairns?"

"Aye, ye missed their arrival. Meet Kenneth and Ivan."

"Are ye well? Are they well?" He wrapped his arms around her and their sons. "They are such wee things."

"We're very well, and Mother had a vision. Both our sons shall hold your ability to shift, and the eldest, Kenneth, also holds my people's fae skills."

"Such a blessing." He kissed her then grinned at his sons. "This day our clan shall celebrate a new beginning."

Aye, a new beginning she would treasure to the depths of her soul, for Gilleoin was now no longer alone. His sons would lead with strength and determination, just as their father led their clan. The heart of the bear would beat strongly within them both.

Chapter 1

Matheson Castle, Scotland, current day.

Isla Matheson gripped the stone windowsill of the briefing room as the dawn's rising sun sent a blaze of yellow and pink shimmering across the treetops and the glassy stillness of the loch. The forest stretched for miles either side of Matheson Castle, providing their shifter-fae skilled clan descended from Kenneth's line with the perfect level of isolation they needed from the rest of the world. That isolation though would never keep her bear shifter mate, a man born to the other clan—Ivan's line—from finding her, not when his senses reared to life when the full moon rose. This was the one night she both feared and desired. For five long years, she'd run, attempting to keep one step ahead of her mate's relentless pursuit. He was strong, but then again so was she.

"I thought I'd find you in here." The door to the briefing room shut with a soft snick and her father walked in with a laptop wedged under one arm. Murdock Matheson was both a seer and the chief of their clan, her only parent and one she loved dearly.

"I just needed a quiet place to gather my thoughts. The full moon looms."

"Speaking of the full moon. I have some new information about your shifter mate." He laid one hand on her shoulder and gave a gentle squeeze. "Are you prepared to listen?"

"Always. Did you have a vision?"

"I did, and from that vision I was able to discover exactly who he is."

"I already know who he is."

"You only know he's from Ivan's line."

"That's all I need to know. He's not from our clan and I'm worried about being the one who sets the prophecy in motion, as well as anxious about losing you." At least the other Matheson clan kept their location as tightly a guarded secret as they did theirs. Even during those times of the month when the desperate need to join with him rode her hard, she couldn't.

"You're in pain and I can see it. Running from your chosen one is difficult. This is a bond that runs to the depths of one's soul, whether you've met him or not." He set his laptop down on the large mahogany table in the center of the room and wrapped one arm around her shoulders. "*Gilleoin's sons will separate when they come of age and rule their own clans, yet there will come a time far in the future when a mated bond forms between the two clans. Only then must Gilleoin's descendants once again merge, and the 'power of three' be unveiled.*" He breathed slowly out. "Yours is the first mated bond to form between the two clans in over eight-hundred years and whether you wish it or not, Gilleoin's lines must once again merge."

"I can't leave you, no matter if I want him." Damn the strength of the mated bond and its unearthly pull on her. She didn't want to leave her father. She was all he had. He needed her.

"Yet your future has been set, and I can't continue keeping you all to myself, even as much as I would love to." He pressed a kiss to her forehead. "Let me show you what I've uncovered.

This is footage taken by a city surveillance camera I was able to download."

"If you believe I need to see it then please, show me." With her heart torn in two, she walked to the table, prepared to face her future even as she ran from it.

"I'll hook this up to the big wall screen." In his navy trousers and tan button-down shirt, Dad powered up his laptop, keyed in a sequence and moments later, the high definition floor-to-ceiling TV screen on the far wall, lit up a solid blue then flashed to the first image.

A city street. The glass front doors of a bank opened and a tall man with shoulder-length locks of midnight-black strode out. A tattooed mark, in the shape of a bear's claw on the side of his neck, gave evidence of exactly who he was. Only the chief's eldest son within Ivan's line—the second-born son—held that mark.

She palmed her dual claw-and-star tattoo hidden low on her hip under her jeans. As her father's only daughter, his only child, he'd marked her with the firstborn's mark. She lifted her gaze. The man on the screen strode along the pavement, his black pants hugging his muscled legs and his white collared shirt stretching tight across his broad shoulders. His bearing and imposing height ensured those walking toward him veered out of his way, then he slowed and stopped next to a sleek red convertible. He opened the door, his long sleeves lifting and exposing the tip of a sheathed wrist dagger.

A slow heat invaded her limbs and spread in a rippling wave through her body. This kind of reaction to her chosen one, she didn't need. "What's his name?"

"Iain, the eldest son of Michael Matheson, the chief of his clan."

"Where's their shifter base located?"

"That I haven't unearthed yet, and last night when I called my government contact, he informed me he couldn't disclose that information, just as he couldn't disclose our location to the other clan." They'd been aware for some time that the other clan worked the same high level government cases that they did. "Although I was informed that your mate has put in several requests demanding further information on us. Of course he's been denied each time."

"He's impatient."

"I'd say he's done trying to track you on the night of the full moon. You're too fast, too quick at running."

"Running is the pits." That tore at her the worst, knowing what she denied them both. The mated pairs within her clan held the closest bond and she'd always desired the same, to be so at one with the man who wished to be the same with her. If only her mate wasn't from Ivan's line it would make all the difference. She didn't want to give up her father or her people. "That sweet ride of his should be easy enough to track via satellite if we go back through that day's images. We don't need to rely on our contact."

"You wish to know where he lives?"

"Aye, so I can stay well away from the place."

"I've already done a search. Iain waited it out at a hotel then traveled under the shield of darkness once he left the city. They're as secretive as we are and remain well under the radar."

"What else have you got on him?" Her father never left any stone unturned once he began an investigation.

"Iain is a triplet and has two brothers, both identical. I discovered that information while searching through the births records. That's where I discovered his father's name and designation."

On the screen, Iain scanned his surroundings then stopped and stared at the surveillance camera mounted near the bank. Gaze narrowed, he looked right at her, his stunning golden eyes shimmering in the sunlight. She could drown in that gaze. So beautiful. Her fingers tingled and she itched to grab him, to remove the space that separated them by the camera lens. "He's definitely my mate. My desire for him is strong."

Slowly, she stepped around the table and stopped before the screen. She lifted one hand, traced along the firm angle of his jaw and over his bottom lip. His tongue darted out, his heated gaze turning to one of promise before he stepped back, eased inside his car, revved the engine and took off with a squeal across the blacktop. Gone, and everything within her cried out at the loss. "It'll be harder to steer clear of him now I've seen his image."

"You've been struggling lately regardless."

"Which city, Dad?"

"Edinburgh, although he could be anywhere by now." He turned his laptop off and the wall-mounted screen went blank. "There's no taming an alpha male's bear, Isla. He's closing in on you and I can sense that."

"There's no taming a compeller either." She was Murdock Matheson's daughter, a fae gifted shifter who held a hypnotic voice none could ignore. She'd confront her mate only as and when she was ready.

"Just remember, your ability to sense him tonight will be different now you've seen him."

"Oh, I'm aware." A desire to tangle with her mate seared through her, left her both wanting and uneasy. She jiggled where she stood.

"I want you to relax." Dad stepped up to her, grasped her hands. "You also need to cease worrying so much about me. Focus only on what you know is the right thing to do."

"I'll try, but old habits die hard." She hugged her father, the one man she loved beyond all reason.

* * * *

After leaving her father, Isla strode to her chamber, opened her desk drawer and palmed her gun. Their work was dangerous no matter the skills they held and even though she'd be on the run tonight, before that time she had an active case to work with her partner, Daniel. Owen and Ewan Mathie were two shifters within a rogue offshoot Matheson branch, one that thankfully held a very weakened bloodline. Those two men, brothers of the same ilk, had killed two innocent people on the night of the last full moon when they'd allowed their bears to roam and now that they'd tasted human blood, they had to be captured and contained. She looked forward to the chase, to ensuring they paid for their crime. It'd certainly take her mind off her mate's chase tonight.

Swiftly, she slid her weapon into the back rise of her blue jeans then strapped on her ankle dagger and tugged her favorite knee-high black leather boots over the top. She swapped her long-sleeved shirt for a cooler white tank top since summer sat on the brink of arrival and her shifter-fae blood ran hotter than mere human blood alone.

Strappy red purse slung over her shoulder, she opened the door to find Daniel leaning against the opposite wall. "You appear ready to roll."

"Just waiting on you." He slung his battered denim jacket over one shoulder and pushed off the wall, his disheveled blond hair falling forward over his brow. "I can't wait to capture the Mathies."

"Me too." She trod down the passageway beside him. "I saw on the latest data that came in that we're heading to Loch Bear."

"To the bed and breakfast right on the fringes of the forest. It's the only place where the Mathies might stay that's close enough to their last known location. Have you got your sweet voice primed in readiness?"

"I do. What about Emma? Will you be able to make it back in time to spend the night with her?" His wife and her best friend had given birth six weeks ago to the first cub conceived in their clan in five years. They were all completely besotted with the wee boy who had the sweetest tuft of blond hair and the most stunning golden eyes. If only their clan births weren't dismally down. It made her decision to run from her mate all the more harder since she was adding to the problem of their people's slow extinction instead of aiding it.

"Emma understands."

"I highly doubt it." Their desire for their chosen one intensified beyond control on this one magical night. It was when their bears rode them the hardest.

"Well, she understands enough to let me go. I also intend to return just as soon as I'm able to."

"When is her next medical checkup?" One of their clansmen held a medical degree and rooms on the first floor, his door always open.

"She's got an appointment today. We're both hoping she'll get the all-clear. Her bear is clawing for its release." A female couldn't shift while carrying a child or in the weeks following her cub's birth, not until her body was fully healed and the Change no longer harmful to one or both of them.

"I'll make sure to drop in and see her once we're back, that's if you let her out of your bedroom." She strolled downstairs then headed around the perimeter of the great hall. Near the fireplace, several of their clansmen lounged on a group of four comfy blue swede couches. She waved out but didn't stop to chat, not when they needed to be away. She stepped outside and strode down the front steps.

Across the keep, a dozen men had broken into groups of two and shirtless, wearing only low-slung jeans or their belted plaid, they battled each other with their swords and shields glinting in the midmorning sunshine. Modern technology had changed the world, but at the heart of their clan, they still adhered to the old ways. And with their shifter-fae blood so strong, the only way to expend their immense energy was with such intense training.

She followed the cobbled path around the side of the keep and walked through the postern gate. In the rear lot, the center's black SUVs lined up in a row, gleamed.

Daniel pulled a set of keys from his pocket and opened their vehicle. She hopped into the passenger seat while he turned the ignition on. The radio blared and she turned it down.

They drove along the winding road, left the sanctuary of Matheson land and joined the thrum of traffic on the main highway. This was the most beautiful land. Rolling fields of heather were awash with wildflowers and the craggy hills of the Highlands called to her very soul.

"Sooo," Daniel drawled, "his name is Iain Matheson."

"Dad told you?"

"I was there when he downloaded the footage. I'm also your partner. There's nothing you can't keep from me that I won't eventually ferret out."

"'Cause you're nosy like that." She smiled. In truth she kept nothing from Daniel and never had. They'd grown up together, tussled as cubs and still did as adults. "Now I need to decide what I do about tonight."

"You're thinking of doing something different to the norm?" Interest flared in his gaze. "You feeling the need to get laid, little sister?"

"Not if Iain Matheson is as annoying as you are to be around." She rested her arm along the armrest under the open window and tapped the black leather. "It's no wonder he's been so persistent. He's their chief's eldest son. I'm surprised he didn't actually find me that first night." She'd waited out in the courtyard, so hopeful that when her mate appeared, she'd be overcome by the bond and finally be able to join with the one man who'd always been meant to be hers. Although none of her clansmen had appeared and that had rocked her soul, and her world.

"A lucky break for sure."

"What did you think of the footage?"

"He's one big bear, but if you need me to brawl with him, I can bring out the claws." His tone was smooth, his grin a teasing one.

"What claws? You keep levitating your opponents then just kick back while they twirl helplessly around in the air."

"Iain's no fae-skilled shifter. I'd have to even the playing field with him and set my ability aside. It'd be the only right thing to do."

"You are all talk." She laughed and squeezed his arm. "There's a very good chance should I ever allow my good sense to fly out the window and let my mate capture me, that I'd get real feisty with you for playing with what's mine. I might even have to take you down."

"You couldn't take me down if you tried."

"Wanna bet?"

"Five bucks says I'm right. I bet I could take your mate down and you wouldn't even lift a finger to help him."

"One hundred bucks says I'm right and you're the one going down."

"I'll stretch to ten but that's it."

"You're clearly worried I'll win. One hundred and not a cent less."

"Fine. I was just trying to save you some money for when you lose."

"Sure you were." More of her tension seeped from her. Daniel knew how to divert her thoughts and lighten her mood.

"Have I ever mentioned how much Emma likes being levitated?" That teasing grin of his was back in place. "I spin her around and have my wicked way as I—"

"No." She flung up a hand. "Too much information."

"Wimp." He chuckled as he motioned toward the gas station up ahead. "I'll pull over here and refuel while you grab us some lunch." He indicated then crawled into the far lane once it had cleared.

She strolled inside, perused the café area with its shelved delicacies and drooled over the offerings. She had a mighty sweet tooth and selected two slices of gooey chocolate cake as well as half a dozen sandwiches to share between them, of which Daniel would eat the lion's share. He always did. Where he packed all the food he consumed though, she had no idea. With two cups of steaming coffee in hand, black and strong, she trod back to her partner and passed him his brew.

He drove and they munched and planned their coming mission. The weakened offshoot Mathie branch only held four shifters and Owen and Ewan could only shift on the night of the full moon, which meant tonight was the night they had to catch them if they wished to ensure another innocent person wasn't harmed.

Hours passed and Daniel weaved along the winding forest road while along the horizon, the sun began its descent. "You need to hurry it up," she told him.

"We're almost there." He eyed the GPS. "We'll make it before nightfall and before the Mathies have a chance to shift. We've got to catch them before they cause more mayhem."

"I've never been this far east before."

"I have, a time or two." He pointed up ahead at a quaint stone cottage nestled within the woods. "There's the inn we're after."

He slowed then pulled into the gravel parking lot. A sandstone cobbled path led to inn's front door with its rustic bed and breakfast sign strung above it. With one finger, Daniel lifted his aviator sunglasses up and surveyed the area. "Nice and remote. The untamed forest surrounding this place would definitely call to their bears."

"Then let's go rope us some big bear." She hopped out, patted her weapon still resting at her back and walked around to Daniel as he holstered his gun under his jacketed arm and straightened his buttery-colored t-shirt over his black pants.

At the hood, he breathed slowly out, his claws slicing in and out.

"You okay?"

"Just fighting the early stages of the full moon. I want my mate." The males always suffered to a greater degree on this one night, their need riding them hard if their female remained some distance away. It wouldn't help that it had been some time since they'd last been able to join as one.

"You got the sedative?" She nudged his arm.

"Sure do." He dug out two vials from his inner denim jacket pocket and gave the deep orange concoction a swirl. After they'd caught the Mathies, they'd ensure they slept until they'd dropped them off to their contact. Owen and Ewan would require containment unlike the rest of the criminal population. Daniel turned in a slow circle, this time sniffing the air.

She did the same.

A trace of smoke puffing from the inn's chimney added a slight taint to the pine fresh air swirling around her. She dug deeper. Beneath the pine, she caught the deep earthy tones of the land. No bears.

She attuned her hearing. Small critters scampered through the dense underbrush and the splashing of water beyond, traveled to her with ease. "There's a river close by."

"But no bears. We'll need to check inside as well as do a wider perimeter search." He set a hand at her back and guided her past a scratched-up mustard-colored Jeep, a white van and a blue sedan.

At the front door, he pressed the bell and waited beside her.

"I'll see who that is." A man's deep voice rumbled through the door. It swung open and the portly gentlemen with a head of gray hair nodded at them. "Good evening, folks. Are you after a room for the night?"

"We are." Daniel slung an arm over her shoulders and

ruffled her long hair. "My sister and I are heading up higher into the mountains in the morning. Do you have any vacancies?"

"The wife has her family staying over for a few days so we only have the one room left. It does have two single beds though, so it's yours if you'd like it."

"We heard." Isla cleared her throat and used her hypnotic voice to its fullest. "That you might have seen two men we're eager to catch up with. Both brothers, their names Owen and Ewan Mathie."

He stared into her eyes, his own clouding over under her compulsion. "They dropped in, and have twice before. They left not long ago to take a hike in the woods. That Jeep in the lot is theirs. They asked if they could leave it there for the night and I agreed. They wanted to sleep out under the stars tonight, although they used the spare room last night."

"Could you confirm that this is them?" She slid a photograph of Owen and Ewan from her pocket and passed it across.

"That's them all right."

Daniel sent her a silent look that said, *Bingo. Now let's find them.*

She smiled at the proprietor. "We'd like to take a look around. I'd appreciate it if you showed my brother the room the two men stayed in while I wander around the backyard. You'll find nothing suspicious about our request and you'll forget you ever saw us after we leave."

"Of course." His glazed eyes focused a little, but her compulsion would hold without issue for Daniel. No one had broken through her ability's hold yet.

She winked at her partner. "I'll take the outside since compelling beats levitation. Call out if you need my help."

"Sure will." He wandered inside with the proprietor.

Setting out, she trekked along the cobbled pathway winding around to the rear of the property. Either side of the walkway, thick lavender bushes swayed in the breeze. She stepped onto the grass dotted with tiny yellow flowers and surveyed the area. The forest butted right up to the rear of the property. She marched in that direction and finally caught the very faintest whiff of bear. Excitement thrummed through her and she picked up her pace and entered the woods. Jogging, she followed the leaf-strewn trail into the dark recesses of the wild. Her bear pushed under her skin, demanding the Change. "Not yet," she urged it. "You've got to wait until our job is done."

Ahead, the trees stood tall and proud next to a fast-moving river and two massive bears clawed a trunk then sniffed, jerked their gazes toward her and snarled.

"Well, hello, boys. I take you two are Owen and Ewan? It's about time we met."

They shoved off the trunk and landed heavy on all fours. Both prowled toward her, their beady black eyes holding only the barest rim of shifter gold on the edges. They heaved up onto their hind legs and roared, drool flying from their jaws.

"Down!"

They bellowed and attempted to fight her compulsion.

"I said—"

A man bounded out of the brush, slung her over his shoulder and bolted along the trail through the trees. Branches scraped her bare arms and her hair flew into her face and obscured her vision.

She shoved her hair back and clutched his pumping arms, her belly thumping into his rock hard shoulder. The ground blurred and the trees whizzed by. She couldn't catch her breath. "W-what are you doing?"

"Getting you far away from those bears." One deeply sensual tone that curled her toes. Now that really shouldn't be happening.

Everything spun and she squeezed her eyes shut. "I can't leave my partner to fight those bears on his own." She shoved her upper body up, looped her arms around his neck and slid down his chest and into his arms. "I want you to—" Whoa. Her heartbeat tripped out of time.

Oh hell. Her mate had found her, and the moon only just glimmered on the horizon.

* * * *

Iain Matheson couldn't believe his good fortune. He'd been out in the woods close to Ivanson Castle when he'd scented her, the one woman he'd been searching five long years for. His bear had gone half-crazy with need and so had he. He only wished he'd been paying more attention to his surroundings. He'd missed catching the other two unknown shifters as they'd made the Change so close by, shifters not of his clan, of that he was sure.

"I—I—" She searched his gaze then blinked as if checking to make sure he was real. "Put me down." Her voice rang with authority, with a sweetly hot demand that curled around his senses, a demand he couldn't ignore.

Gently, he lowered her to her feet, set her before him. A compeller. This wouldn't be easy.

"I see you hold one of the rarest of the fae skills." He'd scoured through what historical information remained on record, even as scarce as it was. Being aware of what he might be up against when he did find his mate, had been a necessity.

"I do." Her golden eyes, so gloriously alive, flickered with defiance and frustration. He'd need to take great care to ensure she didn't use her skill against him. Now that he'd finally found her, he didn't care to lose her. Or at least not before he knew exactly where she lived.

"You've been very hard to track down." Hard was an understatement. If only his clan held the knowledge of where the original House of Clan Matheson resided, but when Ivan had left his home, so many centuries ago, so too he'd taken the knowledge of their location and kept it from even one soul. Arms crossed, he listened for any movement through the woods. Not one noise, other than the chirping of birds and buzzing of nighttime insects. "You said you can't leave your partner to fight those bears alone. Who's your partner and who were those shifters? They're trespassing on my clan's land."

"Owen and Ewan Mathie. They're brothers who are predators through and through, and must be stopped, tonight, before they can harm another. I left my partner behind. Daniel won't be happy that I did." Her cell phone jingled and she hauled it from her jeans pocket, pressed the speaker and answered. "Daniel, the Mathies are in the forest, about a quarter of a mile to the north of the inn."

"Not anymore they're not. I chased them, but then they backtracked to the inn and took off in their Jeep, right after they slashed one of our tires. I'm changing it now. I'll never be able to catch them with the head start they've got. Where are you?"

"With Iain." She eyed him, sexy narrowed gaze and all.

"Well, that would explain why you left me in such a hurry. Can't control your little bear, eh?"

"She's contained, but my mate isn't."

"You owe me a hundred bucks, Miss You-can't-play-with-my-bear."

"You're not even here for me to stop your bout of playing."

"That makes no difference. You removed him from my field of play."

"He removed me."

"You still lost." A clanking sounded down the line as if her partner had dropped a wrench. Daniel grunted. "Stupid sucky tire. I've almost got it changed."

"Where do you want to go from here, Daniel?" Isla asked him.

"I'll update the chief and form a plan. For now, you do what you need to and we'll talk again in the morning. I'm not leaving here until I know exactly where we need to head. We'll contain the Mathies, one way or another, and soon. Very soon."

"I'll talk to you first thing, or call me sooner if you need to."

"Wait." Iain seized her hand before she could hang up and memorized the numbers on the screen, both hers and her partner's. "I'll talk to you tomorrow too, Daniel."

She glared at him and hung up before Daniel could answer. "You've really tossed a spanner in the works."

"Lovely to meet you too."

"Don't try and be funny." She muttered under her breath as she tucked her phone away then paced the trail in front of him. Softly, she sighed and stopped. "I'm sorry. I'm not normally so rude. It's just this isn't the way I ever envisioned meeting you, and right now I'm currently frustrated. I don't mean to push that frustration onto you." She blew out a long breath then extended her hand. "The name's Isla."

"Nice to meet you, Isla. I'm Iain." He slid his fingers around hers, her skin so warm and soft. Releasing her hand took a whole lot of effort. "Would you care to take a walk? Have a chat and all?"

"It'd be a nice start. Thank you."

"We'll follow the trail." He set a hand at her back and steered her along it. The last rays of the sun shimmered across the darkening sky then disappeared. The full moon hung heavy and low within a blanket of black, its brightness lighting their path along with a glittering array of stars. "I apologize for making you lose your catch. I wasn't aware we had rogue bears on our land."

"Catching them is Daniel's and my current assignment." Her gaze softened as she looked at him. "Honestly, I'm sorry I was so abrupt. I try not to be rude to people I've just met."

"I surprised you. That's clear to see. Tell me a little about yourself."

"Not much to tell. I'm as elusive as they come."

He needed more information than that, and he intended to push as hard as she'd let him. "Have you got any family?"

"Of course. Apart from my entire clan, I have a father. He's the chief and seer of my clan. Murdock Matheson. I'm his eldest, his one and only." She looked ahead along the trail. "You must live close by to have caught me this early on in the evening."

"It appears you've come straight to me this time. Ivanson Castle is just around the other side of Loch Bear."

"So I get to meet you and your entire clan at the same time?"

"No, not if you don't wish to. Just me if that suits you best."

"Just you for now. That I can handle." She shivered as the breeze picked up. It blew her glossy brown locks about her bare shoulders and caused goose-bumps to rise on her arms.

"Here, allow me warm you up." He shrugged his jacket off and held it up for her to slip her arms into. She didn't hesitate to accept his offering. She pushed her hands into the long sleeves of soft black leather and pulled the front edges of his jacket together, covering the white tank top she wore over her jeans.

"Thank you. I wasn't expecting to go for such a long jaunt this deep into the forest." She lifted the collar over her nose and breathed deep. "Mmm, you smell good."

His bear had him leaning in. He buried his nose in her hair, dragged in her sweet vanilla scent. It swirled around and intoxicated him, made him want to pick her up and sling her back over his shoulder all over again. Instead, he gently rubbed her arms then zipped his jacket up and enclosed her completely within its warmth. "Feeling a little less frustrated now?"

"A touch less." She slanted her head, her gaze questioning. "I have no intention of leaving my clan, even though you've found me."

"Is that why you've run from me all these years?"

"My clan's numbers are dwindling. There are far fewer mated pairs than ever before and when I discovered you weren't from my clan, I'd never felt such sorrow. I've let them down."

"So by running, you decided our fate before you'd even given me a chance to prove myself." He stroked a finger under her chin and his bear rumbled in delight at the sheer softness of her skin—so creamy and smooth. "I would never keep you from your kin, Isla, nor do I ever intend to in the future. There must be give and take between mates, and more so between you and I since we come from separate clans."

"You're serious?" Her tone held disbelief. "You won't insist I leave my people to join with you?" She inched closer, touching the tips of her boots to his. Those long legs of hers, encased in dark blue denim, showcased every delectable curve from her pert bottom to her knee-high leather boots that hugged her slim calves.

"That's right."

"Then I'm free to go?"

"You're free to leave whenever you wish, but if you go, then I go with you."

"There isn't a chance you'll abandon your clan to join mine. You're the eldest son of Ivan's line." She lifted one hand, traced her finger over the bear's claw on his neck.

"You seem to know more about me than I know about you, and I'll only ever speak the truth with you. I'd never leave my clan, but so too I'd never demand that you leave yours. I'm open to negotiation, to ensure we both receive what we need to from this bond. I'm not an enforcer with a steel hand."

"Is that right?" She arched one cute brow, rather teasingly.

His mate was feisty and strong, both qualities he admired in any woman, as well as qualities he'd hoped his chosen one held.

"And what is it you'd like to receive from this bond, my mate?"

"You. I desire the bond and all that it entails, but I want the sharing of lives, including that of our clans."

"I'm not really that great of a catch. I can be a little unruly, rash, indecisive, and a complete pain in the butt, or at least that's what Daniel always says. I'd be running in the other direction if I were you, and count yourself very lucky you got away."

"I'll never run in the opposite direction from you." Unable to help himself and needing some form of touch that was so important to shifters, he rested his hands on her hips. "There is a lot a man learns during the chase. You hold great strength, are incredibly smart and have completely captured my attention."

"Are you flirting with me, Iain Matheson?" She slid her hands over his. "Because if you are, I like it."

"You've already proven to me that you're dedicated to the ones you love by not wanting to leave them."

"You need to stop with the flowery words." She smiled, so beautifully it lit up her eyes.

He drew her closer, until if he bent one single inch, he'd be able claim her lips and the kiss he so strongly desired. "Tell me the first thing you've learnt about me during the chase."

"Yesterday, I discovered you visited the bank in Edinburgh and took off afterward in a very sweet red convertible. My father had a vision and captured some footage of you, the first I've ever seen. I've also had the chance to admire your very fine looking butt while swinging over your shoulder. I could still take you though, and knock you for six, and all with my voice alone."

"What else have you got?"

"You've got two brothers, both identical to you."

"And their names?"

"No idea. Tell me about your family." Her curiosity must be eating at her the same way it ate at him.

"My parents are mated, and my brothers and I are tight, very tight. Their names are Finlay and Kirk and we hold a brotherly bond that allows us to sense each other's feelings."

"Interesting." That cute eyebrow shot back up. "Are they mated?"

"They are, but like me, they still search for their chosen

ones."

"Well, their chosen ones aren't from my clan. There aren't any more unmated females of the right age other than me, and I'm not the sharing kind of girl. I'm yours alone. What's their search been like?"

He almost purred at that declaration.

"Rather otherworldly. On the night of the full moon, they're led to where they sense their mate is, yet there is nothing and no one about."

"And they haven't given up their search?" She gripped the sides of his short-sleeved shirt, fisted the black cotton in her hands.

"Not once, and they never shall. The drive to find their women is too strong, as it has been for me." He pressed a kiss to the top of her head, needing an even deeper kind of touch, which would likely only get worse as the night continued on. "It's getting cold out. Let's keep walking."

"To your lair?"

"Aye, to my lair." He steered her along the winding upward trail, her pace slower than before, and not in a nervous don't-want-to-go-with-you kind of way, but as if she was more relaxed, or perhaps curious. Her attentive gaze kept switching from the trail ahead to him.

Before long, they left the trail behind and emerged before Ivanson Castle, the thick stone walls of the keep rising like an impenetrable fortress in the dark. "This is the home of my ancestors and has been since Ivan's day. You also have my word you're free to go at any time, provided I go with you."

"I'm going to keep you to your word."

"My word is true, always has been and always will be." He gestured toward the two-story gatehouse where battlements topped fortified walls and cameras mounted on the top of each crenelated corner sent surveillance footage directly to the guards inside the control room. "Are you prepared to see where our bond shall lead us?"

"That all depends on what you expect from me tonight."

"All I desire is to get to know you. You've nothing to fear."

"It's not fear that rides me. This moment marks a huge change. Nothing will be as it was before the moon rose tonight." She touched her chest then his. "Do you feel it? Our bond already strengthens. I'm quite content to be around you, not nervous or hell bent on running in the least."

"I do feel it, and I promise we'll take whatever is to come, just one day at a time." He caught her hand, curled his fingers around hers and looked deep into her eyes. "I need you, Isla. Meeting you is all I've longed for."

"You seem far too agreeable." She searched his gaze then nodded. "All right. I can do this, but just you and me as promised. We'll talk some more, get a feel for each other and where we stand."

"Thank you." His mate was prepared to talk and for that he was most grateful.

He escorted her through the gates and across the inner courtyard toward the side entrance where they could bypass the great hall and surrounding rooms where his family would be. Through the darkened passageways, he led her then up the tower's side stairs and into his chamber. Quietly, he shut the door. "Take a seat. I'll have you warm in no time. There's an attached bathroom if you have need of it."

One with no window and only one door. He could safely allow her out of his sight when she had no means of escape. He'd meant it when he said she wouldn't be going anywhere without him.

"I'm fine for now, but thanks for the offer all the same." She ambled across to his narrow window and with one finger, parted the navy drapes and peered out. "What were you up to in the city the other day?"

"I take care of the clan finances and such. Traveling to the city is a regular jaunt, one you are always welcome to join me on. I'd be sure to make it fun, in and amongst working the figures and monitoring our land and stock holdings." On his knees at the hearth, he tore bark from a log, removed his wrist dagger and struck his flint then blew on the sparks. Flames flickered and he tossed a block of peat on top. He snuck a look over his shoulder when she continued to remain quiet. Her watchful gaze moved about his chamber, took in his large fur-covered bed then returned to him. "Ever been to the city?" he asked her.

"I'm not a city kind of girl." She stepped closer, raised her palms to the flames. "I prefer the wilds of the Highlands, although I'm curious to learn exactly how you'd be sure to make it fun for me?"

"You'd have to come to find out." He rose and dusted his hands against his jeans. She didn't live in the city or the higher populated area surrounding it. At least he had another question answered. "How dangerous is your work?"

"I never leave on assignment without a team member, which is usually Daniel. Even though our clansmen are highly skilled, we never take the chance of losing one of our number." She backed up and perched on the lid of his engraved wooden trunk at the end of his bed. A glorious smattering of freckles sprinkled across her cheeks and nose, made him itch to touch them, to move closer and trace each one.

"Are you warming up?"

"Aye, I am. Thank you." She unzipped his jacket, folded and laid it beside her. "I didn't even sense you close tonight, not even one hint of a warning."

"You should never feel uneasy when you sense me close by." Not liking the distance she'd created, he closed the gap between them and crouched at her feet. "Has your father aided you in eluding me all these years, being that he's a seer?"

"No, I've managed to elude you all on my own. I also

wasn't paying a great deal of attention on you tonight, not when my mind was on my current case." She lifted a hand, cupped his cheek. "Honestly, it's been a burden running from you, and I know my father had hoped I'd soon one day stop."

"Your father sounds like a man I'd like to meet." As much as he'd detested her need to run, he'd also admired her ability to keep one step ahead of him. No more though. Now it was time for them to join together, to complete the bond—when she was ready—and merge their lives into one. All he'd ever anticipated was finding his chosen one, and for their clans to finally have some much needed hope. "We have so much to talk about."

"We do."

His mind reached out, brushed against hers and found a solid barrier. A barrier he didn't care for. Pushing, trying to find a way in, he couldn't halt his mind from demanding the merge that would invariably allow him a constant link of communication to the one woman who was always meant to be his.

"I can feel that." She scrubbed a hand across her forehead and grimaced.

"I'm sorry. The need to forge a merged link with you is strong. Everything within me desires it, to be a part of you, to speak with you at ease, no matter where you are." He hauled his mind back. The last thing he wanted to do was to harm or cause her any pain. He slid one hand around the back of her head and gently drew her forward until their foreheads touched. Her warm breath whispered across his cheeks and calmed a little of his mind's need. "Has the pain receded?"

"It's going." She rubbed her forehead against his.

"Earlier you said you were your father's eldest, his one and only. What of your mother?"

"She passed away not long after I was born. I was schooled right alongside Daniel and a few other close friends within clan walls, my father close by."

"I'm sorry about your mother. That must have been terribly hard for you and your father to lose her so soon in life." His parents were rarely apart, found any great length of distance separating them difficult, no matter their merged link. They were each other's confidants, lovers, their one-and-only. A relationship he desired with all his heart. Her admittance also brought with it a great deal of understanding. She and her father must be tight.

"It's never easy for one who is mated to lose their other half. Dad's commitment to raising me though kept him from losing it. His clan also needed him, and we rely on his wise judgment and strength." She looked deep into his eyes. "I've always felt torn, Iain. He's given up so much to remain with me, and I've felt driven to give him the same commitment in return."

"You harbor guilt?"

"Guilt, and love, and kin. They're a powerful combination."

"For the past five years, I've ached for what could be and for what's always remained just beyond my grasp. But I want you to lay any guilt you feel aside. Going forward, we start fresh, with no recriminations or blame. There is only us, and how we intend to live our lives from this moment forth." Being with her was all he'd longed for, and now the chance was here, he wasn't about to lose her before he'd ever had the chance to know her. "Apart from your father, who's your next closest?"

"Daniel."

"Does he have a mate?" The man better have.

"Aye, and a wee son who is only six weeks old. Daniel holds the fae skill of telekinesis. With his mind alone, he can levitate objects or people."

"Then I thank you for the warning." He didn't doubt that as close kin, Daniel would be as protective of Isla as her father would be.

"You'll need the warning, although I'd never let Daniel hurt you." She touched one fingertip to his chest then slid it between two of his shirt buttons and stroked his skin. "You're very warm, almost too warm."

"It's been a few days since I last shifted. Being in the city prevented me from doing so and when I returned, I was busy preparing for the chase."

"If you need to shift now, feel free to do so."

"I'll only shift if you do."

She shook her head. "I want to talk to you and I can't do that if I shift."

A good sign. His bear settled at the thought.

"Every mated pair in my clan knew each other for years before the mated bond drew them together." She popped another of his buttons, eased her entire hand fully inside and palmed his flesh. "We don't have that same benefit going into our mated bond. I don't want to move too fast, even though I can't help but want to touch you. The need is strong."

"As it is for me, and we'll take things as slow as you need to. We'll find the right balance. I like having your hands on me. It's soothing." It calmed him as nothing else could. "Touch me, wherever and however you please."

"You are far too amenable."

"I've never made the offer to another soul, just you." He rested his hands on her hips, slid his thumbs under the hem of her white tank top and stroked her smooth skin. "And if I move too fast, rein me back in. I'll understand." Gazing into her eyes, he shared the words emblazoned deep on his heart. "What belongs to me is now yours, including all that I am."

"You are also far too sexy for words." A teasing smile lifted her lips. "Does that inclusion of what belongs to you go as far as your convertible?"

"The key is in the top drawer of my dresser and the car is parked in the lot out the back. You have to take the postern gate to reach it, but again, you're not to leave without me. That is my one and only stipulation." He caressed her back and pressed her closer. Five years of searching for her, of feeling incomplete and now she was here, right where she belonged. He closed his eyes as another wave of deep desire rushed through him. "Thank you for allowing this kind of touch. I need it, bad."

"The urge to bond is strong." She lifted her arms and wrapped them around his neck. "The full moon is attempting to get its way."

"We'll control what will or won't happen this night, not the moon." He sank his hands into her hair and luxuriated in the slide of her dark silky locks slipping across his wrists and forearms. His bear fairly purred for more and carefully, he unleashed a touch of his control, lifted her up, scooted with her onto his bed and laid down beside her, one leg firmly over hers to hold her in place.

"Talking of control." She touched her lips to his ear and whispered, "Stay very still. No more moving for you." Hypnotically compelling words.

"You don't need to compel me if you don't wish for me to move." Damn it. He couldn't move a muscle. She'd restrained him, fully and completely. "How often do you use your skill?"

"When and as needed, but I just couldn't help myself right now." She nudged him onto his back and perched beside him then lifted one foot and unzipped her boot. She tossed it onto the floor then unzipped the other.

"How long does the compulsion last?"

"Do you mean when will you be able to move?"

"Exactly."

"Until I free you." She winked, shuffled to the end of the bed and unlaced his boots. She removed and propped them next to hers then crawled back up and straddled his hips. With one sensual move, she slid a weapon from the back rise of her jeans, checked the safety and leaning over him, placed it on the bedside table.

His fingers twitched, the bone-deep need to touch her

clawing at him.

"Don't try to fight the compulsion. It can become painful if you do."

"At least you're making yourself comfortable and not racing out the door." Thank heavens for that.

"I just needed a moment, and you did say I could touch you, wherever and however I pleased. I do tend to take things literally." She traced along his lower lip, reached the center then swept back to the corner. Her golden gaze swirled with desire, the same fierce emotion raging through him. "When I first saw your image from the footage my father downloaded from the city, I touched you just like this." She stroked along his lip again and he nipped her finger then sucked it inside his mouth. Slowly, she leaned in, her lips a mere breath from his. "If you're in any pain, then tell me."

A surge of heat flared down his spine, rolled into his groin and hardened his cock. He groaned as his shaft rose and tried to spear through his pants. "Ignore that."

"I've been celibate my entire life. I couldn't ignore any part of you if I tried." She stroked down his chest and along his waistband. "Would you like to move?"

"You compelled me for a reason, and not just to see how I managed not being able to move. I obviously came on too fast. I won't have you fear me or my touch in any way. If this is what you need to do to feel more comfortable, then I can readily accept it."

"I'm not uncomfortable, not in the least." She pressed one hand to his chest, right over his heart. "I want your touch, Iain. I want to get to know you, to see what I've been missing out on since the chase began. I know my father would want that for me too. I release you from your compulsion."

Even though she had, he remained perfectly still, his greatest desire now to unravel each and every intriguing part of her.

* * * *

Iain didn't move even though she'd released him from her compelling command. She smiled. "I like you. You've surprised me at each and every turn so far tonight."

"I like you too. I also want to smother you in my scent. Is that permissible?"

"Of course." Her heartbeat picked up its pace. She wanted his scent all over her, for both her and her bear. She couldn't hold back that need.

Gently, Iain rolled her onto her side then facing her, smoothed one hand over her lower back. Fingers splayed wide, he rubbed his body against hers, ensuring his scent encased her, just as he'd done outside in the forest when he'd slid his jacket off and zipped her securely within it. She liked it. A lot. Particularly when he slid his fingers underneath her shirt's hem and stroked along her waist.

She nuzzled his neck, right over his tattoo. "Your mark is stunning."

"Do you have any distinguishing marks yourself?"

"I'm the first female in my line to receive one." She lifted her tank top a touch and nudged her jeans down an inch to expose her hip and the small tattoo of the claw-and-star mark symbolizing her dual shifter-fae blood. "Since my mother passed away only a week following my birth and my father knew I'd be his only child, he honored me with the mark."

"It's beautiful." He stroked one thumb over it.

"Thank you." She tucked her top back down and played with the last two remaining buttons holding his shirt together.

"Take my shirt off if you wish."

"Are you reading my mind?" She desperately wanted to. Skin to skin contact was necessary between mated pairs and she was no different in her desires even though she'd run from him.

"I'd like nothing more than to read your mind, but it'll keep."

"You're doing a fine job even without the merged link." She lengthened one claw and sliced the buttons away then peeled the soft cotton back and licked her lips. His wide chest, so heavily muscled held a smattering of hair, the same dark shade as his head and a teasing trail led down and disappeared inside the waistband of his black jeans. She shoved his shirt off his shoulders, exposed his muscled arms and thick biceps. So beautiful, and all hers.

"Isla." He groaned, his golden gaze heating to a molten hue. "You may need to compel me again. Your touch is only going to encourage me to want more."

"What kind of 'more' would you like?"

"I want to kiss you."

"A kiss would be nice." She didn't want to turn him away, not when she too craved what she'd been forced to give up for so long.

"Then I have your permission?"

"You do."

He dipped his head, licked her lower lip then grinned. "You taste good."

"That's all you want?"

"Hell no." He covered her mouth with his and licked her tongue. She swayed forward and he captured her lips in a deliciously scorching kiss, his hard body a powerful heat that carved warmth into her own. Mmm, he tasted good, so good. She melted against him, reveling in his scent as it swirled around and embedded itself deep within her.

Even as she'd run from this bond, she'd still yearned for it. She melted further into his touch. His breath whispered softly across her tongue, an incredibly sensuous caress that had her urging his lips apart and deepening their kiss to capture more of his essence.

This was so very right, and she indulged as her need for more rushed through her. She plunged her tongue inside his mouth and drank in his delectable taste, welcoming the raw intimacy she'd never experience with another. Only him. He was the one destined to be hers. "Oh goodness." She pulled back a touch. "I really love the way you kiss."

"And I love the way you respond." He caressed her sides, roamed down and scooped her bottom. Then he kissed her again, so deeply, so wildly, that their breath mingled as one and completely scattered her thoughts.

"More, Iain."

"What kind of more do you want?"

"For you to mark me."

"Are you sure?"

"Very sure."

He rolled her onto her back and rose over top of her. He nibbled along her jaw and down her neck. She arched into his touch as he scraped his teeth over the sensitive skin where her neck and shoulder met.

A scorching heat shimmered through her and pooled between her thighs. She wanted his mark, just as she wanted to give him hers. "Do it."

"I'm just enjoying the ride leading up to it." He slid one finger under her shoulder strap and eased her tank top away from her neck. A low rumble vibrated in his chest as he pressed himself against her and sucked on her offered skin. Then he teased her with his tongue, stroked one hand down her throat, over her chest and curved his palm around her breast.

"I can't wait any longer." Her pulse raced, so fast.

"Neither can I." He bit down and arousal hit her hard and fast. She clutched his shoulders, her nails digging into his flesh.

He licked her skin, soothing the spot where he'd bitten before lifting his head and looking into her eyes. "Are you all right? Your skin is so flushed."

"I liked it, a lot."

"As did I." He rolled her into his side and pulled her tight against him, his hand firm on her thigh as he tucked his top leg between hers and ensured they touched along their entire length. Slowly, he slid her hair back from her shoulder and eased her other top strap to the side.

"Are you going to bite me again?"

"Aye, the same time you're going to bite me. Since completing our bond must wait, we both need this." Head lowered, he cupped the back of her head and drew her mouth to his neck. "Am I right? Tell me if I'm not."

"You're right." She gave into the deep need burning within her, sucked his skin into her mouth and razzed his flesh with her teeth. Her nipples hardened into tight points and she rubbed her breasts against his chest to ease the ache.

"Now," he growled.

She clamped down on him and he did the same to her. Pleasure coursed through her, sweeping her away on a tide of wonder. He was hers and she wanted everyone to know it, and this mark she'd given him would ensure it.

"Isla." He hissed out a breath and rocked his leg between hers.

"So good," she murmured, a tight need for more building deep inside her.

"What do you want? Tell me and I'll deliver."

"Make—got to have—I just need more."

"I've got you." He gripped her thigh, pressed his jean-clad leg even higher into her crotch and urged her to move on him. Sweet heaven. The seam of her jeans pressed into her clit and she couldn't help but rub harder against him.

Dizzy and breathless, she kissed him, with all the passion and intensity taking her over and he rocked his leg harder into her and made her gasp as white-hot pleasure struck her. It ricocheted outward from her core and hardened her nipples even further. He'd driven her so swiftly and completely over the edge and she soared as bright lights sizzled behind her closed eyelids.

"Oh goodness," she panted as she slowly came back down. "That was totally unexpected."

* * * *

"It was also beautiful to see." Iain stroked Isla's hair as her breathing returned to normal. Watching her soar skyward from an orgasm he'd given her had made him deliriously happy. She was so responsive to his touch and he adored it. He nuzzled her neck, her scent below sweeping up and over him. So intoxicating. "Are you all right?"

She opened her eyes, blinked and cleared her dazed gaze. "I can't believe you just made me come, while I'm still fully clothed." She rubbed the spot where he'd bitten her in a slow circle with her thumb then palmed the mark and held it to her. "No more biting me tonight. I'm not sure I can handle another episode like that without wanting to tear your clothes off you."

"That was hardly a warning if that was your intention." His cock throbbed for release. He'd never had sex before, but he'd certainly watched a few interesting movies and right now all he wanted to do was slide her jeans down her legs and feast on that part of her that had wept for him.

"I can see what you're thinking." She tapped his nose. "You need to stop it."

"You're torturing me." He cupped her face in his hands and kissed her, his mouth moving in a slow exploration that left them both ragged for breath when he pulled back. It would take every ounce of his willpower not to succumb to this desperate desire he had for her tonight.

It would surely be one long evening.

One he never wanted to have end.

He'd found his mate and his soul rejoiced in the fact.

"Tell me what you're thinking," she murmured.

"My soul is in heaven."

"Likely right alongside mine after what you just did to me."

"Aye, what happens to you, happens to me." He grinned,

completely taken by the woman before him. The days ahead shone with a brilliance he couldn't wait to explore. With her. Only with her.

184

Highlander Heat

Highlander's Castle, Book One
Highlander's Magic, Book Two
Highlander's Charm, Book Three
Highlander's Guardian, Book Four
Highlander's Faerie, Book Five
Highlander's Champion, Book Six

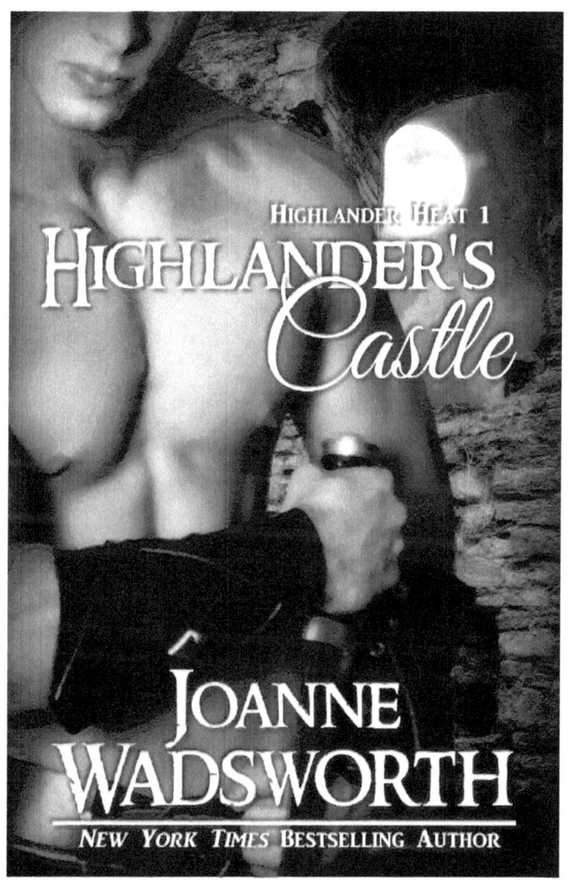

The Matheson Brothers

Highlander's Desire, Book One
Highlander's Passion, Book Two
Highlander's Seduction, Book Three

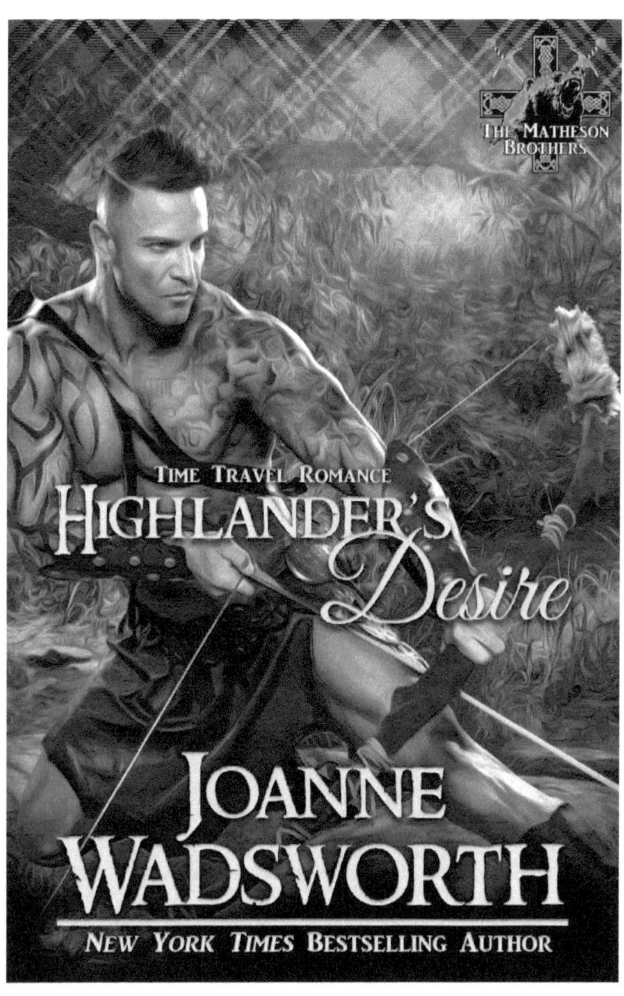

The Matheson Brothers Continued

Highlander's Bride, Book Seven
Highlander's Caress, Book Eight
Highlander's Touch, Book Nine

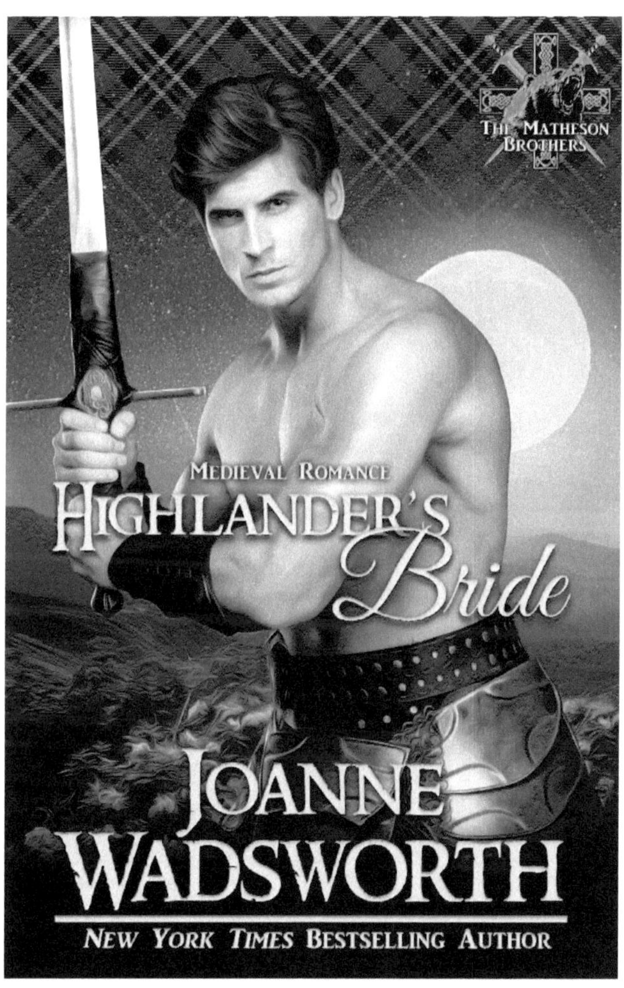

The Matheson Brothers Continued

Highlander's Shifter, Book Ten
Highlander's Claim, Book Eleven
Highlander's Courage, Book Twelve
Highlander's Mermaid, Book Thirteen

Princesses of Myth

Protector, Book One
Warrior, Book Two
Hunter (Short Story - Included in Warrior, Book Two)
Enchanter, Book Three
Healer, Book Four
Chaser, Book Five

JOANNE WADSWORTH

Billionaire Bodyguards

Billionaire Bodyguard Attraction, Book One
Billionaire Bodyguard Boss, Book Two
Billionaire Bodyguard Fling, Book Three

JOANNE WADSWORTH

Joanne Wadsworth is a *New York Times* and *USA Today* Bestselling Author who adores getting lost in the world of romance, no matter what era in time that might be. Hot alpha Highlanders hound her, demanding their stories are told and she's devoted to ensuring they meet their match, whether that be with a feisty lass from the present or far in the past.

Living on a tiny island at the bottom of the world, she calls New Zealand home. Big-dreamer, hoarder of chocolate, and addicted to juicy watermelons since the age of five, she chases after her four energetic children and has her own hunky hubby on the side.

So come and join in all the fun, because this kiwi girl promises to give you her "Hot-Highlander" oath, to bring you a heart-pounding, sexy adventure from the moment you turn the first page. This is where romance meets fantasy and adventure…

To learn more about Joanne and her works, visit
http://www.joannewadsworth.com